RUTH

By the same author

The Complete Guide to London's Antique Street Markets

Nineteenth Century Romantic Bronzes

Under the Hammer: The Auctions and Auctioneers of London

Dealing with Dealers: The Ins and Outs of the London Antiques
Trade

RUTH

JEREMY COOPER

Hutchinson
London Melbourne Auckland Johannesburg

© Jeremy Cooper 1986

This edition first published in 1986 by Hutchinson Ltd, an imprint of
Century Hutchinson Ltd, Brookmount House, 62–65 Chandos Place,
London, WC2N 4NW

Century Hutchinson Publishing Group (Australia) Pty Ltd,
PO Box 496, 16–22 Church Street, Hawthorn, Melbourne, Victoria 3122

Century Hutchinson Group (NZ) Ltd,
PO Box 40–086, 32–34 View Road, Glenfield, Auckland 10

Century Hutchinson Group (SA) Pty Ltd,
PO Box 337, Berglvei 2012, South Africa

British Library Cataloguing in Publication Data

Cooper, Jeremy, *1946*—
    Ruth.
    I. Title
    823′.914[F]   PR6053.056/

    ISBN 0-09-167110-8

Photoset by Rowland Phototypesetting Ltd
Bury St Edmunds, Suffolk

Printed in Great Britain by
Anchor Brendon Ltd, Tiptree, Essex

PART
I

1

Ruth worked in silence, perched on a faded pink cushion at one end of the duet stool. The embroidered seat dipped in the middle, like Mrs Cornish's apple and blackberry pies, and strips of jute webbing hung down below the fret-carved apron; hence the cushion. Ruth was leaning forward, sticking out her bottom, her woollen skirt pushed up by the bulging satin cushion. She had a biggish bottom and a broad back, and her shoulders rose and slowly fell, the trough of each exhalation so deep she seemed to need reminding to breathe again.

Ruth's commitment to the job at hand was total: it always was, to the things she did well. All morning since shortly before eight Ruth's world had been confined to six square inches of canvas at the bottom left-hand corner of a work she sometimes called 'my masterpiece' but more often referred to as her cross. A cross she was glad to bear; the cross she believed might mark her grave. In four weeks time, at the end of May, it would be three years since Ruth had first turned her still-life gaze in upon herself and started work on – on 'Thy Kingdom Come', as she called it in the end.

This morning she hoped to finish one of the easier bits, the briar rose, leafless for winter, which grew between the toes of Queen Guinevere's questing beast. Ruth had grown fond of this pre-human creature, waddling away out of her picture space from behind the Queen's knees. He was too funny to be frightening and however monstrous she tried to make his dactyl head, investing the veined nostrils and cadaverous eyes with the worst kind of animal threat she could imagine, she could never take him seriously. His scaly chest, puffed out and hanging down between claw-paws, reminded her of Archibald, Mum's mandarin duck. It was not how a questing beast *ought* to be nor how she had wanted him to be, but there was no changing him now. Ruth turned round from time to time and looked up at the dead briar strands decorating the minstrel's gallery. Two summers ago she had gathered great armfuls of rose trailers and woven them through the balustrade. Every other day she had sprayed her creation with rainwater in an effort to prolong life in the cut flowers, but their petals had still curled sepia brown and fallen to the floor. The leaves also withered and fell; the stems first turned golden then grey, the thorns pale yellow then white, seeming to grow larger, sharper, like the unsheathed claws of a feral cat.

Ruth put down her brushes and palette and rose to her feet in front of the canvas, not so far now from completion. She held out her left hand, palm upwards, and extended her index finger. She looked down at her own hand, and up at Sir Lancelot's outlined against a waning moon. She pushed back the sleeve of her pullover and placed her hand against the picture, the inside of her forearm the musty white of linen lain overlong in wardrobe drawers, blue veins marching crazily backwards from her wrists. Sir Lancelot's hand; reaching, beseeching. Her own hand; cold in the moonlit void of the picture space. Turning away, she walked over to the gallery and unhesitatingly pressed her extended finger against the hooked point of a briar thorn. The skin stretched taut and gave way, the sword of the rose slipping into her body. Ruth gasped and pulled back her hand, holding it above her head, a prick of bright blood quickly swelling dark and round. Eyes closed, she brought her finger to her mouth, tongue reaching out to touch the host: the Blood of our Lord Jesus Christ which was shed for thee – drink this, and be thankful.

Ruth sucked at the damaged finger; then wrapped a paint-splashed rag around the wound, and returned to her work.

The music room, for twelve years now Ruth's studio, was the grandest room in Kenton Priory, opening out through floor length windows onto a glazed verandah and the garden beyond. The house itself faced the wrong direction, northwards into the side of the hill and away from the long views over Watham Moor to Glastonbury Tor. It stood, tradition told, on the site of an ancient priory endowed and dedicated by King Arthur to the blessed memory of Sir Ector le Chalibaille, his first and shortest lived Lord High Almoner. There being no evidence of this earlier dwelling, Ruth's father – the late Mat Harrison – used to insist the story was 'all medieval mumbo-jumbo'. Still, the flintstone finish to the front and west wings of the house, and the outlines of towered porch and vaulted music room made an ecclesiastical impression on first-time visitors. Turning in towards home through the eyebrow entrance, gateless for as long as she could remember, and walking down the tree-lined drive, Ruth herself had often felt like a returning pilgrim – if only from a ten minute stroll to collect their mail at the village Post Office. In contrast, Ruth's side of the house was simply dressed in unadorned red brick continuing along the walled garden and round into the yard with its reassigned stables and the favoured back door. Twinkle, Ruth's oldest and closest friend, was the only local regularly to use the front door of the Priory – because it was the nearest to the studio, and because the fluff and feed in the yard made her wheeze. Years before, Twinkle's mother – a potter in the village – had made Mat Harrison move the hens into the orchard; but they had never settled there and were soon allowed back into the yard.

Mrs Harrison no longer noticed the mess the hens made. Nor did Ruth, not really; at least, she never said anything. Mum loves her hens so, she would tell herself. And without Mum there is nothing: only darkness.

The big kitchen, the scullery and the gun room were tucked away at the back of the house, the dining room lying end-on to the studio and looking out onto the rose garden. On the floor above, the main bedrooms fitted themselves around an E-shaped landing. At the back, Ruth's small room pointed over the gabled barn roof towards Dad's lake and the sedgemoor beyond; in winter she had a clear view of the ruined chapel on the Tor. At the other side of the hall from the studio was a dreary cavern of a room which Mat Harrison, hard as he had tried, had never managed to make his family use convincingly. Ruth could be in there on her own in the middle of a summer's day, fetching a book perhaps or a photograph album, and sadness still wrapped itself around her heart. The Georgian furniture and lax rococo bibelots seemed to snigger behind her back. She loathed Dad's sporting pictures too: 'A Brace Apiece'; 'Full Cry' – of tally-ho huntsmen leaping Leicestershire fences; 'Glen Kyllachy'; and the three Herring mares: poorly executed symbols of rural respectability. To Ruth, the drawing room meant an *Ode to a Nightingale* recited to dinner guests who would not listen, and Dad pinching her arm to make her say goodnight nicely.

The tip of Ruth's tongue appeared at the upturned corner of her large mouth, and stuck there. She was at work again.

The light in the studio was perfect, a soft light flooding in through the long east windows of the verandah. Wisteria used to cover the whole length of the verandah's glass roof but years ago Mr Cornish had cut the branches back at this point. It had been such a relief to them all when Ruth revealed her extraordinary gift for painting; they had watched with amazement, and with joy, as she progressed from empty drawings of houses on graph paper, blocked out in poster paint, through meticulously coloured tracings from the *Magazine of Art*, to beautiful little still-lives in oil, of birds' nests, shells, dried flowers, all the usual things. The summer before Dad died Ruth's first two pictures had been accepted at the Royal Academy: a small canvas, 'Abandoned', of sundry oddments scattered on the studio windowsill; the other, 'Spring Love', a simple posy of primroses, their stems wrapped in silver foil, lying on a bed of moss. They were so proud of her, Dad especially, and when she complained of the wisteria blocking out her light he had ordered the virile old branches to be cut away, the stumps to be daubed in pitch. Ruth was very upset at the time and for two months afterwards had refused to use the French windows onto the verandah.

She wondered what Dad thought of the big picture. Her masterpiece, her cross. At prayer she begged for Dad's approval.

The unmanageable canvas, five foot wide by four foot high, was supported on two easels. Ruth used the duet stool only for the bits at the bottom, and normally worked on her feet, half-leaning against the tall artist's stool Twinkle had found for her in a Shepton junk shop, the friendly one beyond the railway bridge. She took up her palette again – one of three, each reserved for a different colour range, with tin containers for oil and turpentine clipped to the side. Her empirical technique was laborious in the extreme. Like a grand-scale miniaturist, she painted with fine sable brushes in liquid colours, creating physically flat images of magical complexity. 'Rossetti's heir', the art critic of the *Western Weekly Gazette* had called her; 'a visionary in the home', Bill Compton of the *Guardian* had pronounced on seeing 'The Martyr's Gate' at the RA, a jewel-like painting of two moth-eaten eighteenth century dolls standing in an upended cardboard box roughly tied with string.

The drawing alone for the new painting had taken Ruth nine months to complete. Transferred to a tracing paper cartoon and pounced through to the canvas, she had laboured a further year over its tonal underpainting, in shades of green: perfect in its limitations, pure and breathless in the monotone. Ruth had waited weeks before daring to overpaint her first colour, the burnt ochre of the halo, a golden dish on which rested her central motif, the isolated head of a man-God-magician: St John the Baptist, Merlin, the King himself, Our Lord. As the work progressed she had decided to leave certain areas green. Mark's dream and Sylvia's dream – interchangeable sacred and profane images of love, circular reflections of the same embracing couple guarded by the angels of birth and rebirth – remained unaltered. Green also seemed to fit the questing beast, and Ruth was just now overpainting the winter briar where it curved up around his puffed-out chest and away into the midnight air. There was a leaf of red cabbage beside her on the table, picked fresh from the vegetable patch, inspiration for an invented hybrid plant anchoring her canvas at this corner, the revealed bones of nature's skeleton an appealing challenge to her skill.

Ruth abruptly stood up and stepped out through the verandah window.

She stood blinking in the sun; a pale lady, at first sight older than her twenty-nine, almost thirty, years and at a second glance much younger – an innocent. Three septic spots stained the skin of her wide forehead. With the exception of her button nose all Ruth's features were full, the mouth especially so, her curled bottom lip often dropping open as she worked, accentuating the dimple in her chin. Hair grew distressingly strong and black on her upper lip, a product of the thirteen-year search for a cure. No one seemed able to say what had suddenly happened to her all those years before; certainly no one was willing to tell her precisely what was still wrong. Ruth sometimes feared they did not really know. 'Your chemical imbalance,' Dr Cardy always called it. 'I think we've got it licked this trip' he would say, time after time.

They were all so kind to her. Everyone tried so hard. And her own dear Dr Fletcher in Eastney, well, he was a saint – there was no other word for it.

It was midday; Ruth turned back into the studio and draped a muslin curtain across her painting. Outside again, the proper path continued straight to the ha-ha at the end of the garden, but Ruth's own well-trodden way led her to the left over some drooping chicken wire and through the spinney. At the stile she stopped, stood still in the shadows. She counted: one, two, three, four . . . all the way to twenty-three before two of the heifers looked up from their noisy tearing at the grass. They all sensed her presence then, and eight black noses turned in her direction, an occasional pink tongue curling up a nostril. Ruth clapped her hands, and laughed – a clarion laugh.

'Caught you!' she shouted. 'Silly Misses!'

The shiny black heifer nearest the stile kicked all four feet off the ground and bucked her back legs, hopping away like a clockwork bronco. Ruth jumped into the field and gave chase, but she quickly tired, and turned to walk slowly up the side of the hill to the crown of beeches, hands pressing on knees to ease the climb.

At the iron gate, secured by swathes of orange baling twine, she paused for breath. Standing there at the base of the crown, Ruth looked down on the Priory roofscape and away to Glastonbury, feeling, as she often did from this vantage point, outside herself. She clambered over the gate and up the turf steps that scaled the sides of the crown, topped by a ring of elderly beeches. She passed between the trees, stepped across the miniature stone bridge spanning the ditch, and measured her usual twenty paces to the very centre of the circle. She sat down on the worn patch of grass and tilted her head heavenwards. Through the circular hole in the leaf canopy – branches reaching out but forever falling short – her spirit soared, up into the blue sky. She felt the warmth of the sun's rays on her closed eyelids and pulled the unwanted spectacles from her nose, letting them fall on a lurex cord against her bosom. She sighed, and smiled.

When Dad was alive he had kept the crown in immaculate order, attacking the chickweed and cleaning out the tiled circumference ditch every winter. At regular intervals during the Easter holidays he and her brother Mark had made solemn inspections of the lawn and, at a certain point, when the ground was sufficiently firm, they would set out the freshly painted hoops and declare the croquet season open. For two years after Dad's death Mark had managed to keep pace with Priory traditions, trying as hard as he could to fill his father's boots. The July tournament had gone ahead, and was won both seasons by Mirabel Fitzgerald, the first year through the kindness of her brothers, the second on merit. But that second autumn Mark had married Sylvia Sayers and run away from Somerset; then at Christmas the cattle had broken down the fence, making a terrible mess of the croquet lawn before they were discovered, wheeling and churning in the mud and covering the lawn with cow-pats. Five years on, Ruth felt the crown of beeches had acquired a wholly different character, more ancient and peaceful, more in tune perhaps with another life, past and future. She opened her eyes. A carefree Mother Shipton bobbed and wove a path between the sunbeams. Ruth got up and tiptoed after the butterfly-like moth. It led her a dance through the long grass before coming to rest on the balcony of Dad's dilapidated gazebo. Ruth held out her hand.

'Come my love. My little beauty,' she whispered. 'Come to me.' The moth squeezed its wings and waggled its antennae. 'Oh lovey, are we purring?'

Ruth reached out to stroke the brown-spotted moth, and away it flew. She sat down on the wooden steps and placed a hand on each breast. They lay small, high and wide, and she pushed them closer together. They were all the wrong shape. She did not know quite what to do or what to think about them. Beneath her Shetland pullover and long woollen undervest she pressed her breasts down until the nipples caught the rim of her spectacles hanging at her neck.

'See better now, diddums?'

She rocked back on the steps, laughing out loud. Peals of unrestrained laughter. Mouth open wide.

Ruth unhooked the latch on the gazebo door and looked inside. She heard a scuffling behind the pile of logs: field mice or a rarer beauty perhaps, a weasel disturbed in his daytime sleep. The rattan chairs were stacked toe-to-tail on top of each other, a disintegrating pyramid of broken legs and dislocated arms, ransacked for nesting material by the animal kingdom of the crown. The iron-girdled croquet box lay there, lid open, rusty hoops and well-made old mallets untidily thrown together. The faded colours of the centre post – in descending order – blue, red, black, yellow. There was a fisherman's stool on the floor, its striped canvas seat torn in two, and a small easel leaning against a cobwebbed window, remnants of summers before the big picture when Ruth had often worked in the open air, safe within the protective ring of beeches, a floppy felt hat pinned to the back of her head. Mark's favourite picture had been painted on the crown, one of the few things he had taken with him from the Priory. 'Green Fugue', it was called: the dusty-green mower standing on the cut-green lawn in front of the newly-painted-green gazebo against the sun-spotted-green leaf curtain, the stage empty after Dad's final exit.

Ruth wandered between the trees, their roots exposed where the earth slipped down the hill – flying buttresses enclosing cloisters, in and out of which young rabbits played at sunset. The exposed roots were slippery, forcing Ruth to extend a balancing hand to the low beech branches on which she had scrambled as a child. Not only as a child, as a girl too, as a young woman even, right up to the day of her collapse three weeks before her eighteenth birthday. Ruth climbed clumsily astride a dipping branch rubbed smooth by generations of bony little bottoms and sticky-soled prep-school sandals. She gripped the strong arm of the beech between her thighs and pushed up with her feet from the ground and down with the weight on her arms; up and down, up and down . . . Ruth stopped and slid off the branch, falling to one knee in her haste and confusion. The husk of a beech nut attached itself to her brown woollen stocking; she bent down to extricate the barbed husk, careful to avoid snagging the wool, and brushed her hand lightly between her thighs.

'God's will,' she muttered. 'Alone He knows.'

Ruth walked back to the centre of the crown, head lowered, the barley grasses pulling at her skirts. She reached the bright patch of sunlight and lay down full length on her stomach, arms outstretched, the warm earth pressed close to her cheek to receive her tears.

Rolling onto her side, Ruth curled up her knees towards her chest and cradled her head in her arm. She closed one eye and gazed at grasshopper height at the blurred borders of the perfect circle; she shut the other eye and drifted off into her favourite dream – of the princess incarcerated by virtue of her own true love in a tall ivory tower, marked today by this very crown of beeches. The walls of her virgin's tower, warm to the touch, were built from great blocks of ivory cut on the curve and exquisitely feather-grained. The walls climbed sheer from the glassy waters of a bottomless moat, the polished ebony draw-bridge destined to remain closed until a scarlet knight rode down the valley from Glastonbury and up to the foot of the tower with the Holy Grail balanced in the palm of his chain-mailed hand. High in the side of the ivory tower, so high that no one on the ground could be quite sure of what they saw, a single window faced east to Jerusalem. Every evening at sunset, when the princess sat at this window and looked out into the black sky, her beautiful face was bathed for one whole minute in a beam of light reflected from the dome of the Holy Sepulchre. One evening many years later – Ruth had not yet decided how many years later it actually was – there was no living beam of recognition from distant lands at sunset, and on the last stroke of midnight the virgin was released from the ivory tower and borne away on the back of a winged stallion to join her Lord above.

Sometimes – not today – the scarlet knight returned triumphant from the Crusades and they lived happily ever after, the drawbridge always lowered, always festooned in multi-coloured bunting.

Ruth left the crown and walked back down the hill towards home. Emerging from the spinney, she heard her mother's call:

'R-u-u-th. Lu-u-u-nch.'

'Coming, Mum,' she shouted back.

Instead of returning through the studio window Ruth walked across the granite gravel drive, circled the giant pampas grass, and entered the back yard.

'Hey! Careful, Mrs C!'

Their daily woman wobbled round the corner on her heavy Raleigh bicycle, a box of gone-to-seed cabbages precariously balanced on the handlebars.

'Ooh, Ruth! Sorry, dearie. Oops, no you don't!'

Though the brakes on Mrs Cornish's bicycle worked perfectly well, they were seldom used. She stopped by putting both feet to the ground, daring the machine to proceed further; as Mrs C was a considerable size and pedalled very slowly the bicycle came to an instant halt, its saddle buried in her skirts.

She grabbed the toppling box and admonished the cabbages, to whom the 'no you don't' had been addressed.

'How are you today?' she continued without breaking breath. 'Lovely steak and kidney just out of the oven. All crispy like you like it. Bye for now, dear.'

'Bye, Mrs C, bye. See you tomorrow.'

Ruth waved at the retreating figure, and shouted after her. 'Bless you!'

Mrs Cornish raised one hand in the air in acknowledgement, veered towards the stream and, straightening up, continued down the drive. Ruth turned into the yard and entered the house through the kitchen door. She washed her hands in the chipped scullery sink, deep enough to drown a cat, the hot tap shuddering from the effort of producing a trickle of scalding water. Mrs Harrison was standing at the window, hands massaging the wooden back of a kitchen chair; she was listening to the radio which stood on the windowsill, half-listening, her pale blue eyes wide open. She relaxed when Ruth entered, her freckled face breaking into a smile. Ruth went over and hugged her, bending to press her forehead into the hollow below her mother's collarbone.

'Oh, Mum,' she sighed.

Mum patted her on the back of the neck, and blew into her ear.

'Come on, Ruthiemoo, eat. Where've you been? We're half an hour late again.'

'On the crown,' Ruth replied, sitting down and tucking greedily into the plate of pie and vegetables waiting on the table.

'You're so silly. Why can't you look at your watch?'

'Forgot.'

'Well, don't forget,' Mrs Harrison remonstrated. 'It's asking for trouble, you know it is.'

Ruth looked up at her mother, a dribble of gravy descending her chin, short-sighted brown eyes bright with false hope.

'Is that what it is, do you think?'

'Of course it is. Dr Fletcher says it'll make all the difference. Worked yesterday, didn't it? And the day before.'

'Can't remember.'

Mrs Harrison laughed, the same kind of laugh as her daughter's, loud and uncontrolled, a surprising laugh for a small woman.

'Ruth!' she exclaimed, and sat down at the other side of the kitchen table to eat her lunch.

Ruth finished one helping and served herself another. She gobbled this too, leaning over the table, her mouth an inch or two above the transparent pyrex plate which she tilted to lick clean.

'I saw a beautiful moth. Beautiful, really. Like you.'

They smiled at each other, endlessly forgiving. Ruth continued to stare, seeing her mother as she really was, an aging wine-soaked widow with an indestructible core: her memories of Dad, and the desire blindly to follow his wishes to the end of her years. Ruth saw the wispy grey hair which had fallen out in brushfuls after Dad's death. She saw the wrinkled mouth twitch between forkfuls of steak and kidney pie, and did not flinch from her mother's watery eyes staring unashamedly back. Mum's colourless eyelashes fluttered, like the wings of the moth.

After lunch Ruth looked in to the studio on her way upstairs for a rest. She removed the muslin veil and turned the canvas towards the garden sunlight. Her eyes travelled methodically from face to face, only one of which was clearly recognisable; the angle of Queen Guinevere's neck and the clean profile clearly identifying her with Mrs Fitzgerald – Mirabel's mother, John, Graham and Conor's mother, and chairwoman, as she insisted on being addressed, of Eastney and Watham Parish Council.

Ruth kissed the air in front of Sir Lancelot's lips, and went up to bed.

2

The Harrisons and Fitzgeralds were thought of as close family friends. They thought of themselves as such too: veterans of twenty-six years' neighbourly exchange, from childhood birthday parties to the brink of middle age, from young motherhood to grandmotherhood. It was an association of habit, of circumstance, a matter of rural convention and convenience. To be any less friendly, they would have had to become enemies.

Except for Ruth; with her it was different. With her everything was always different.

As the weekend of Conor's wedding drew nearer, the Fitzgeralds came to occupy more and more of Ruth's thoughts. Whole afternoons drifted by as she stared into the semi-night of the big picture, seated on the art-school stool, arms crossed: clenched. Remembering.

Conor, the last of the Fitzgerald litter, was six months younger than Mark and less than a year older than Ruth herself. Log-limbed and credulous as an adolescent, he had burst into late flower at Pembroke, confounding his Harrow School horoscope with a first in Archaeology and Anthropology. 'Fitzgerald M C K got a first, did he? What a waste,' was the verdict on the Hill when they heard the news. Conor was already an area supervisor in British Waterways; a soft man, ripe for marriage. John, his eldest brother, and Mirabel, of course, had both been married from the Lees, and Vicky's parents were given little choice in the matter. The embossed invitation to the third Fitzgerald wedding at Wells Cathedral rested behind the bracket clock on the kitchen mantelpiece announcing to Ruth the end of an era, the passing-out parade of all but her into adulthood.

Ruth did not mind being left behind, at least, not in the usual way, for so many of those things which stirred the sentiments of others – the death of a family pet, a plane crash in the Alps with the loss of three hundred and sixty-five holiday-making lives – seemed to bypass Ruth's emotions. 'God's ways are not our ways,' she was often heard to say in the calm face of inexplicable human suffering, her own as well as others'. Different things ignited Ruth's deepest feelings, and, once alight, the fire burnt with a heat which consumed her completely. There was nothing she could do to control the flames, and at such times she would retire to her small room with its view across the valley and lie down in her bed by the window, hugging her knees and rocking gently against the pillows, silent eyes staring at the Tor; a whole day, sometimes two days, sometimes three. Eventually the fire died down leaving Ruth a useless burnt-out wreck, too weak to leave her room for twice as many days to follow, but able to read at least, and to draw, and to think of being better. First, though, Ruth always sought to find outward expression for her emotions: bravely, trusting in God, and in the world outside.

The newly-weds-to-be had three lists: one at the General Trading Company (their breakfast and dinner services, drinking glasses, lampshades etc), another at Liberty's (bed and table linen, towels, luggage, and household oddments), and a third at Gorringe's in Bath (for the locals – kitchen equipment and useless knick-knacks). Mrs Harrison had written off for all three, a source of endless merriment to her and Mrs Cornish as they pottered about the Priory in the mornings.

'I should get them the electric coconut shredder, Mrs H,' Mrs Cornish would call out as she prepared the vegetables.

'Midnight blue *not* coffee brown,' Mrs Harrison would say when they passed each other on the stairs.

On the Monday afternoon of the wedding week Ruth sat at her lopsided bureau in the studio and tried again to compose a letter to accompany Conor's drawing. She was pleased with the drawing. It said as much as it possibly could. Words were much more difficult.

How do you thank someone for marrying someone else? Would he understand? He *must* understand. He had to.

Ruth found herself glancing back over her shoulder again, yet again, to the time before her illness. To the time when she had seemed much the strongest of them all.

Did he remember dancing classes?

The TA Drill Hall in Shepton: cream-painted brick, artillery green woodwork, and the flaking crest on the wall. Duckboards in the mud where they waited for Madame Micklejohn. The hurrying clatter of high-heeled boots on the pavement at the other side of the hedge.

'So sorree, cheris. Iz 'aff past alreadee?'

The disinfected chill of the changing rooms where they hung up their anoraks and put on dancing pumps – Conor had pumps too, funny tartan slippers secured to his outsized feet by black elastic rugger garters. She and Twinkle and Mirabel rushing to press their spreading teenage bottoms against the lukewarm radiator near the piano. Mademoiselle Feverre, as Madame called her – actually Miss Feather, Ruth had discovered many years later – cracking her knuckles and practising scales. The boys forming a huddle at the other end of the room. Except for Andrew Heath, with his winklepickers and terylene turtleneck, who invariably came over to offer them a stick of gum. Their giving him a hard time made no difference: at the Simpsons' Christmas party Mirabel let him touch her breasts beneath her dress.

Ruth smiled now at her memories. Smiled at the clear recollection of the way she used to shove Conor round the corners in the foxtrot, her sight-lines restricted by his grey-clad chest, his chin bumping across the top of her head when he misinterpreted her directions.

And the day he took her fishing.

She was shocked when he had first suggested it. It seemed such a strange idea.

'Don't tell Mark though, will you?' he had made her promise.

'Oh no!' she had replied, fully aware of her brother's views on girls and fishing.

Conor was a different person with a rod in his hands, slick and subtle, and totally alive. He found her a sheltered spot at a bend in the river and she watched, mesmerised, as he worked the banks either side of her. Now and then Conor looked up, and waved. Before going home he lit a fire of dry twigs and they talked while the gutted rainbow trout grilled in the embers. They talked about everything and anything.

She remembered him saying he hated boarding school and confessing, shyly, how much he admired her for refusing to leave home.

'Brave? Not really,' she had replied. 'I was frightened.'

She remembered describing to him her feelings as she waited for Dad to come and collect her from Cadenham – an hysterically angry twelve-year-old beating her bruised fists against the locked dormitory door. And the journey home to the Priory. Dad and she singing in the car: 'There were ten green bottles standing on the shelf, ten green bottles standing on the shelf, and if one green bottle should accidentally fall, there'd be nine green bottles standing on the shelf. Nine green bottles . . .' Dad had promised never ever to send her away to school again.

'I bet it's great at Shepton High,' Conor had said. 'Better than Harrow any day.'

'Don't be silly, Con. I'll never get to Cambridge, and you're bound to.'

'Yes you will, Ruthie. We both will. You'll see.'

Poor Conor, he still believed in her. Even now. Would he never give up? What more did she have to do before they let her rest?

If only she could cut the threads and set him free – set herself free. Were the words not there? Adult words to loose these childhood bonds?

Ruth took another sheet of cartridge paper and began to write, in her beautifully controlled italic script.

My dearest Conor – she wrote.

I wanted so much to be worthy of your faith, and I have failed.

You who have never failed me deserve more. But I am not able. Please forgive me.

This drawing is for you and for your dear Vicky. It will I hope find a small space that is its own in your house in Exeter, which one day I hope to visit. Not a grand place but an important place, for it is a guardian drawing.

From me it wishes you great happiness in and through your love of Vicky and hers of you. It is impossible to know what destiny holds for us, but at these great cross-roads of our lives I think we must make the choice and then trust. I remember you once talked of utter trust in relationships, and may this be yours. Perhaps it will undergo many metamorphoses but I am sure the vision you behold now will never die, nor leave you. You are just so worthy of each other.

You have great gifts, of nature and of ability, and far to go. There is only one weapon to fight with and that is love. And never forget that one day you are destined to become the very stuff of which your dreams are made. Not to experience joy irrepressible, but to be it.

Even in my weakness, in years to come I hope that if ever you need me I will be able to show in action my deep affection and regard for you both.

My fondest love to you and Vicky.

I remain yours ever, Ruth.

She folded the thick paper and lodged the letter in a pigeon-hole of her bureau. Ruth smiled. It was a lovely letter – clear and calm and beautiful. Two weeks it had taken to write, off and on. Worth it, though, for Conor.

Two days before the wedding Sylvia and the children arrived by car at the Priory, in time for tea. Little Pippa was to be a bridesmaid. There were dresses and bonnets and shoes to try on, and the rehearsal at Wells the following morning, and Auntie Ruth's wonderful stories to listen to in bed. The big painting remained untouched, shrouded in muslin, one good month away from completion, three bad.

On the Friday evening Ruth drove over to Bath to meet Mark off the London train. The train was late. Mark looked puffy around the eyes, his long face twisting into a restricted smile when he caught sight of Ruth.

'Hello old thing,' he said, letting her take the case as he searched his pockets for the ticket. 'Where're we parked?'

'Dad's place. Are you alright?' she asked.

Mark was handsome, in an undemanding kind of way. His

older-looking but younger and dumpier sister reached up to feel his forehead. He leaned away from her touch.

'Sure. Crowded train. That's all.'

Ruth handed Mark the car keys and followed him through the barrier.

'How was the stag party?' she asked once they were safely out on the Radstock road.

'Great fun. Lots of singing. Oh yes, great fun.'

Mark seemed about to go on, then stopped, frowning.

'Well?' Ruth prodded.

'Well what?'

'Tell me all about it, you goose!'

Ruth wriggled impatiently in the passenger seat of Dad's old Jaguar, slapping her hands on the veined grey leather. Mark laughed – he suddenly seemed to relax, and began to describe the Fitzgeralds' party the night before. He kept his eyes fixed on the road ahead as he talked, accelerating confidently out of the bends in the high-hedged country lanes. Ruth turned her head and stared at Mark, her pale face flashing in the headlights of oncoming traffic, concentrating hard on each crumb which fell from Mark's lips. The whole scene slowly formed in front of her bespectacled eyes, as though she was there in person . . .

The only girl at a stag party. What an honour! She wore her dark green velvet dress with the lace collar, and treated herself to a Knightsbridge hairdo, Duchess of Kent style . . .

'Where is the Belfry exactly?' she asked, interrupting Mark's monologue.

'West Halkin Street, off Belgrave Square. Private Club, of course. I can tell you, I've never . . .'

She was five minutes early and asked the taxi-driver to drive round the Square a couple of times before drawing up at the cross-battened door of the dining club. The doorman was dressed in brocade breeches, tails and a riding hat, like a coronation coachman.

'Good evening, Miss Harrison,' he said as he helped her out of the taxi.

Cocktails were taken in the ante-room at the top of the spiral staircase with a view through to the large octagonal room where dinner would be served, in the Belfry's belfry. Cocktails? Or was there champagne only? Anyway, Ruth asked for champagne. She engaged in – and won – an argument over insecticides with Conor's father, congratulated John on becoming a QC, and listened with interest to Ranald Mostyn-Morley exchanging Lloyds gossip with Mark. At dinner she sat between Conor and Mark; there were sixteen people in all, two at each side of the vast Victorian table. Beneath a glass dome at the centre of the octagonal table stood a musical automaton. Ruth reached out and pressed the ivory lever. Three Turkish musicians jerked into life, nodding their papier-mâché heads, rolling their eyes and waving their instruments in pretended harmony with the hidden cylinder music. Above them, a trapeze artist in a star-studded leotard ventured bravely across the wire. On arriving at the other end the acrobat whirled around, the mechanism whizzed and clicked, and off he set in the other direction. Ruth laughed . . .

'It was terribly funny, it really was,' Mark was saying. 'I'd no idea the old boy was up to it. Then John got up. Strictly in order, you know. And he . . .'

Ruth declined the red wine and Conor kindly ordered her a tumbler of iced Malvern Water, with a twist of lemon. She commented on the Piranesi prints hanging on the magenta walls, and praised the celery soup. After the roast duck, but before the profiteroles, Ranald, Conor's cousin and the best man, proposed the health of the groom and called for a verse 'the Irish way'. Giving Ruth a secret smile of resignation, Conor rose to his feet.

'On your chair, boy,' Mr Fitzgerald insisted.

Conor sank a glass of burgundy and climbed onto his chair. Surreptitiously Ruth placed a steadying hand on his ankle as he launched into an impassioned rendering of Yeats' *Innisfree*.

He sat down, well-pleased with himself, and squeezed her knee beneath the tablecloth. While coffee was being served Conor summoned a song from his father. Mr Fitzgerald made an unconvincing show of modesty before delighting them all with his ten stanza version of *Mrs McGinty*. Then it was John's turn, and after him Graham, each son playing his required role in the family ritual . . .

In the dark, tears rolled down Ruth's cheeks.

'When did Cornish weed the drive last?' Mark asked as they passed through the Priory's gateless eyebrow entrance.

'Oh Mark, *please*!' was all Ruth could trust herself to say in reply.

Next morning, the day of the wedding, Ruth woke at six. She could hear Pippa singing to herself in Dad's old dressing room. Ruth got up, dressed quickly, and went downstairs to boil a kettle. In the kitchen she finished off the macaroni pie, cold from supper the night before and, with a cup of tea, she swallowed the first of her four dosages of pills, laid out by her mother on the mantelpiece. The cats were scratching at the door; Ruth let them in, filling their saucer with milk. A puff of June mist followed the animals in, sure sign of a hot day to come in the enclosed watery domain of Glastonbury Vale.

Conor's drawing was already wrapped and the letter sealed, waiting in the studio. Ruth let herself out through the verandah windows and set off on the familiar two-mile walk up behind the crown of beeches, across the shoulders of the two terminal hills and along to Lee Farm and Lee House, closeted together at the other side of the valley.

Mrs Fitzgerald was in the kitchen.

'Ruth dear, how lovely. Con!' she called down the passage to the dining room. 'It's Ruth. She's got something for you. Go on in, do.'

'May I?'

Ruth ran off along the worn stone flags of the passage towards the dining room; just as she reached for the handle, Conor poked his uncombed head around the door.

'Hi, you're up early.'

'So're you!' Ruth replied, giving him a friendly cuff on the chest. 'I've got your drawing.'

'About time.'

Conor took the parcel and began to untie the string, placing the briar rose bouquet on the sideboard.

'I'll read the letter later,' he said, knowing that was what she would prefer.

Inside the brown paper package Ruth's drawing was encased in a layer of tissue.

'Here. Let me.'

Ruth tore away the covering and held up her work for inspection.

'There! What do you think?'

Conor pulled at the lapels of his tartan dressing-gown, retying the cord at his waist.

'It's not quite what I expected,' he said.

'Extraordinary. You've never done anything like that before,' commented Mrs Fitzgerald, who had joined them, and was pouring her husband a fresh cup of coffee. 'It's very beautiful though,' she concluded.

Ruth was delighted.

'Yes. I'm happy with it actually. What about you, Con? You've got to like it too.'

'Yes I do. I will, I'm sure. Just got to get used to it.'

He gave Ruth a brotherly hug and continued with his breakfast.

Mark, Sylvia, Pippa and baby Alice left the Priory at two, an hour and a half before the service was due to begin. Mark deposited his ladies at the Pembertons, where Vicky and her parents were staying, and went on to rendezvous with the other ushers at the cathedral. John gave them all their orders, charging Mark with the responsibility of shepherding the ailing Lady Abrahams to her place – aisle seat, fourth row, groom's side. The only outsider in the group of Somerset ushers was Vicky's cousin, a dapper young man in ribbed morning coat and fertile cravat. It was a wonderful sunny afternoon and crowds of trippers milled about the cathedral close waiting for a sight of the bride. John strode purposefully down to the lich-gate and back, brushing bystanders from the path.

'Better watch out for gate-crashers,' he warned his cohorts, all now button-holed in lily-of-the-valley.

'No hat, no seat,' Vicky's cousin suggested.

John eyed him suspiciously, his intended reply curtailed by the late arrival of the two trumpeters, requisitioned from the Welsh Guards in Monmouth.

'Ah, you're here. Follow me,' John said and led the way up to the clerestory, directing one bandsman to either side of the nave.

Guests began to arrive: in twos and threes at first, the women tugging at the buttons on their gloves as they ran the tourist gauntlet of T-shirts and tennis shoes, the later guests in a steady stream of unembarrassed silk and taffeta, polka-dots and candy-stripes, and butterfly buckles.

Mrs Harrison and Ruth were amongst the last to arrive.

'Are you sure I'm alright?' Ruth asked again as they hurried across the market square.

'Fine, darling.'

Mum stuck out her chin defiantly, stopping to push the ungainly black beret further back on her daughter's head.

'More like bagpipes than a beret. Rosa "who" wore these things?'

A blue-rinse tourist dawdling on the pavement in front of them dropped her ice-cream cone in shock at Ruth's bellowing laugh at her back.

'Oh Mum! Don't! Rosa *Bonheur*. The Landseer of France,' Ruth screeched.

The two women gripped one another's wrists in the fierceness of their mirth, bending their heads crazily together.

They stopped again a little further on to wave to Vicky and her father in the limousine, and were shooed towards the cathedral by John.

'Come along, Mrs H, we're running late.'

Still chuckling, they hurried hand in hand across the close, to be met by Mark's disapproving frown at the West Door. He led his mother and sister down the aisle towards their reserved seats in the third row from the front on the Fitzgerald side.

'We'll sit here. Don't worry,' Ruth whispered, pulling at his arm and pointing to one of the gaps on the left.

Mark was forced to stop and explain the seating system.

'I know!' Ruth replied, getting still more agitated. 'But there are so few on Vicky's side. I'm going here. Come on, Mum.'

Mark hesitated, and gave way: heads were turning, and he could see the Bishop and Lance Hibbs, their vicar, already greeting the bride. A blast on the organ gave the trumpeters their cue and the great Gothic vaults of Wells Cathedral echoed and re-echoed with the heralds' call to celebrate the marriage of Miss Victoria Sally Field to her beloved betrothed, that gallant gentleman Mr Michael Conor Kilbane Fitzgerald.

Ruth dropped to her knees and buried her head in the sleeves of her outlandish costume. Oblivious to the progress of the service, absorbed in her own ardent prayers for the lives and souls of Vicky and Conor, she prayed for their children and for their children's children, heaping blessings on unborn heads. Ruth finally raised her eyes at the sound of Reverend Hibbs' familiar voice in a short address from the chancel steps, and accepted her mother's hand at her elbow, helping her up.

Dear Reverend Hibbs, he was such a sweetie: when he knelt down to pray the soles of his shoes glinted in the candlelight, like knightly armour. He lived with his widowed sister, bred boxer dogs, and kept a beautiful album of pressed wild flowers. People could say what they liked about Lance Hibbs, he was a holy man, a man of God, she just knew he was.

'. . . and in the five years I've been at Eastney, the Fitzgerald family has shown me personal kindness beyond measure. This truly is a Christian family and today's union of Victoria and Conor is most surely blessed, and confirmed, in heaven above.'

'There you are!' Ruth mouthed to her mother.

After the service there was one queue after another. A queue to leave the cathedral. A queue for official photographs at the lich-gate. A queue in the car park behind the shopping centre. A queue of traffic sweating in the sun on the narrow road to Lee House. And the last queue, in through the front door to shake hands with the bride, groom, parents, and parents-in-law, a quick look at the opulent display of presents and out through the French windows to a slightly soiled marquee. Many guests took their champagne and canapés out onto the lawn, or along the generous paths of the orchard, the grass cut low for the occasion. In the paddock at the end of the orchard Mr Fitzgerald's prize lambs and mothering ewes turned tail at the colourful crowds of visitors.

Mrs Harrison ignored the signs directing her to park in an adjacent field and drew up in the back yard. They skipped the reception queue too, and hurried into the marquee: Ruth was seriously late for her four o'clock round of pills and calories.

'Hot sausage roll, Ruth?' asked one of the village women serving at a long table.

'Anything yes. Lovely, Mrs Mac,' Ruth replied, as she piled her plate high with food.

Mrs Harrison located a dish of roast chicken legs and stuck a drumstick straight into Ruth's mouth.

'Delicious,' she said, eating one herself. 'We'll have a couple more of those.'

They hurried to the nearest table where Ruth demolished shrimp canapés by the handful.

Mrs MacAndrew placed four cups of tea in front of her favourite ladies. 'Good to see Ruth eating well, isn't it, Mrs Harrison? She looks the picture of health. A proper picture. I'll say.'

With her second cup of tea Ruth swallowed the bright plastic capsules her mother produced from a handbag.

'That's better,' she announced, and turned to face the throng.

Ruth rubbed her mouth with a wet paper napkin, then her spectacles, and placed them on her nose; she stared ahead, registering for the first time the hundreds of people.

Where did they all come from? What did they all do? Why? Why here?

Why everything?

Ruth spotted Twinkle in the crowd: as so often in the past, her friend's presence brought instant release from her struggling thoughts, drawing off the worst fears and leading them safely away.

'Twinkle! Over here,' Ruth shouted.

Twinkle waved a thin arm in the air. Her son, Gabriel, was walking now, and she bent down to take hold of his hand as he tottered across the uneven floorboards of the marquee.

Loyal lovely Twinkle, Ruth continued, to herself. Silent in suffering, humble in triumph. If only I could learn to be more like you. I'm no good. No, I'm not. If you really were me instead of you in my place you'd soon see. I'm bad, Twinkle. I am, I am. Useless. What have I ever done for you? Nothing. I can't even look after myself. I'm no use to anyone. I never will be. He has cast me into the pit of darkness. Has shut me away for a thousand years. Salvation and glory and honour and power unto the Lord our God, for true and righteous are His judgements.

Twinkle and Gabriel reached the table.

'Gabs-a-Babs,' Ruth cooed, gathering the child into her arms and laying him across her shoulder. 'Who's a beautiful boy? Who's my beautiful boy?'

Gabriel squealed with pleasure and beat his mittened fists against her back. Twinkle sat down, ruffling her spiky hair with gloved hands, protected like her son's against the seasonal ravages of eczema.

'The date and stilton sandwiches are delicious. You must try one.'

'No thanks, Mrs H.'

'I don't know what these are. Taste like sandwich spread. But they couldn't be. Not here!'

'Oh Mum, don't!' Ruth snorted.

Twinkle shook her head in familiar disbelief at yet another of the Harrisons' private jokes.

And after a shared joke, the usual flight of fancy into a world of their own, Ruth's face turned away, her mother staring straight ahead, seeing the same scene in their minds, from different points of view. Teddy bears' tea parties in the Wendy House at the end of the garden in Chaucer Drive; coffee breaks in the mobile library; family picnics at Chawton Woods on precious, sunny Bank Holidays. The ribbed glass jar of sandwich spread on the top shelf in the kitchen cupboard, reserved for special occasions.

'The jars were so pretty. Dad kept his collar stiffeners in one.'

'Before I was born?'

'Of course before you were born, dear. When I was a little girl. Grandpa, not *our* Dad.'

Baby Gabriel opened his mouth and soundlessly deposited a half-digested sausage roll onto Ruth's beret.

'We had sandwich spread on Sports Day at Miss Pilk's, didn't we, Twinkle?'

'Did we? Oh Gabriel. Look what you've done to Jo's hat.'

'We did, you know. Here.'

Ruth handed the baby back to Twinkle and pulled off her beret, wiping it on the table cloth. She was already racing away again in thought and feeling, far away from Conor's wedding, back to her earliest recollections of the move to Watham.

Twinkle wasn't Twinkle then. She was still too young for school. She was Sandra. The perfect china doll, Dad used to call her at tea in Mrs Fare's studio. Sitting near the kiln for warmth in winter. And Ruth was still Ruth, not Jo. That all

31

came much later, with the Nativity Play at Miss Pilkington's kindergarten.

Twinkle, twinkle, little star, how I wonder what you are. My best friend, my best friend: that's what you are.

'I love you, Twinkle,' Ruth said out loud.

'I love you too,' came the relaxed reply.

The marquee had filled up. Bodies and sounds pressed them into their canvas corner. The tea-urn steamed. Mrs Fitzgerald's hat, a feathered fez, bobbed above the heads of the crowd. It was hot and airless inside the marquee and the filtered sunlight cast unnatural shadows on the faces of the guests. Mrs Harrison had turned to the champagne, and waved away approaching friends: 'Yes, fine thanks, Gillian. We're just recuperating for a moment. See you later.'

Ruth sat with her hands in her lap, chin resting on her chest, eyes lowered. Released from the beret her hair fell untidily onto rigid shoulders. Twinkle was feeding Gabriel from a jar of baby food, with her fingers. Ruth opened and closed her mouth, like a fish out of water.

'You can't love me,' she insisted.

'Why can't I? I do anyway.'

'No! I don't deserve it.'

Beads of sweat burst through the caked make-up on Mrs Harrison's face; she looked beseechingly at Twinkle. Twinkle patted Gabriel on the back and rocked gently in her chair before replying.

'I'll love you if I want. It's got nothing to do with whether you deserve it or not.'

Ruth raised her head and stared at Twinkle.

'Do you think I deserve your love?' Twinkle continued. 'You do love me though, and I'm glad of it. Gabs is glad of it too. And we like loving you back, don't we, Gabs?'

The baby looked at his mother, head lolling, and then at Ruth. He seemed to stop and think, wondering how to respond. With a smile and a gurgle he opened his chubby arms wide and reached for Ruth – too young to fear a friend.

For a moment Ruth's face was drained of expression; it was only a moment, a tenth of a second, less, before she sighed and held the baby to her body, tears streaming down her cheeks. Mrs Harrison took a gulp from her refilled glass of champagne and dabbed at her face with a lipstick-stained handkerchief; in her less demonstrative way, Twinkle also looked relieved. They were both happy to let Ruth cry herself out of the immediate crisis.

'Oh Gabriel,' Ruth exclaimed when she had calmed down. 'Your Aunt Ruth's such a feeble creature. Tcha! What'll we do with her?'

'Take her home,' her mother said.

'Oh yes, Mum! Do let's. Right now. Please!' Ruth pleaded, like a child. Unnecessarily, for Mrs Harrison was already on her feet and squeezing past the tea-urn.

Ruth gave Gabriel back to Twinkle and hugged them both, too hard, for the baby took fright and began to yell. Twinkle stroked her friend's cheek and Ruth stumbled off after her mother.

'I want to say goodbye to Con,' Ruth muttered as they emerged into the sunshine.

Mrs Harrison failed to hear and pushed on through the wedding guests. Ruth stopped. She stared at the ground, scarcely moving a muscle; saliva dribbled from the corners of her mouth. This time she half-screamed, half-groaned: 'Mum! I've got to see Con!'

Her mother turned and was at her side in five hurried steps. She took Ruth by the arm and propelled her into tottering strides across the lawn, massaging the back of her neck with a practised hand.

'Of course we'll see Conor, darling. Of course we will,' she soothed.

The nearest men turned on their heels and walked away, sensing a level of feminine distress beyond their powers to comfort, scared they might witness worse. Mirabel, who had heard Ruth's cry from the orchard, rushed up and took the other arm. They guided Ruth to a bench in the shade of a giant oak.

'Shall I get some water, Mrs H?' Mirabel offered.

'No need, she'll be alright in a moment. Look, Ruthie, it's Mirabel. Don't make a fuss now, there's a good girl.'

Ruth raised her head and gazed at Mirabel as though she was a great distance away, a shadow at the edge of perception. Mirabel did not flinch and the two women, friends since early childhood, sat face to face: Mirabel smiling; Ruth crawling perilously through the blackness. Ruth's face was blotched and heavy, drug-swollen and battered from within, a face barely recognisable from her dancing-class past. Mirabel had changed too, less dramatically but no less painfully perhaps; from careless to careworn, from lover of many to wife of one, from growing to dying. Ruth's large mouth lay open and she breathed heavily. She licked her lips and tried to swallow. She blinked and swallowed again, a smile of recognition finally breaking through into her dark eyes. Without lowering her gaze she fumbled for the spectacles at her neck, and put them on.

'That's better, back again,' Mirabel said in a voice which curled up optimistically at the edges.

Ruth leant her forehead against Mirabel's bare shoulder, leaving her mother to find the words.

'I should've known it would be too much for us and gone straight home from Wells. Such a pity. She's had a wonderful year. Best ever.'

'Yes? Terrific. How's the big picture coming along?'

Like the rest of them, Mirabel never questioned Mrs Harrison's reports of perpetual improvement between the setbacks. If the mother herself was so sure, how could they dare doubt? Everyone wanted to believe the best; it absolved them from responsibility, justified their unwillingness to interfere.

'Paul Furness says it's a masterpiece. Said he'd give anything to be able to paint like our Ruth. Him an ARA! I couldn't believe my ears.'

'Terrific. Ruthie, isn't that great?' Mirabel said, lifting Ruth's head from her shoulder and pulling her friend's hair in play.

Ruth grabbed Mirabel's hands in both of hers.

'I had to come,' she said. 'I had to. Con would never've forgiven me if I hadn't tried. God is merciful, from Him nothing is hidden. Our weakness is His strength. You mustn't lose faith, Bella. Bellissima. Life changes. You can't stop it. Not even you. New joys will come if you let them. I know they will.'

Mirabel recoiled from the burning intensity of Ruth's emotion. She tossed her head and jumped to her feet, smoothing with jewelled hands the wrinkles in her dress at the top of her thighs.

'Are you sure she wouldn't like a glass of water, Mrs H?' Mirabel asked, as if Ruth was suddenly somewhere else.

'No, dear. We'll just slip away quietly. Apologise to your mother, won't you? And tell Mark we'll see him when we see him. No need for supper tonight,' she added, with an attempted laugh.

Mirabel caught herself waving at the backs of the two women as they retreated round the side of the house. She was unwilling to feel sorry for them, to pity them. They had each other, exclusively and unreservedly. The giving and receiving of such love between mother and daughter made up for everything, surely.

They'll never know, Ruth promised herself. No one will ever know. How could they?

I wouldn't want them to.

The pain. The unbearable pain. It's in me. I must keep it there. No one else must know. It's safe with me; in my world it can do no harm, only to me. Give it to me, I'll take it away.

Away from them all.

It's my duty. I mustn't shirk my duty. There's no way forward, or back. Up or down. I can carry it no further.

That's far enough – this time.

The pain cannot be described. Not in their words.

How could they understand?

No sound was heard from Ruth's room the next day until early in the afternoon: at two she was awake and quickly out of bed, sitting on the chamber pot.

Ruth shoved the pot back under the bed and drew the curtains. She climbed back beneath the blankets. The narrow stained-oak bedstead was raised on blocks of wood so that she could see out of the window without lifting her head from the pillow. She watched the swifts building castles in the air and marvelled at the patterns of light cast by the aging poplars' young leaves, fluttering in the breeze like migrating butterflies. It was difficult to believe the lemon-green leaves were actually fixed to the branches: she expected them to fall away, setting her eye free to follow her thoughts down Dad's path to the sedgemoor, over the waters of the lake, through the buried streets of the ancient lake village and up the sides of rounded hills to Glastonbury. Her first thoughts of the day often made this journey.

Ruth's room was small and overfull. She had chosen this particular spot in the house to make her nest on being rescued from boarding school. Much had been added since, and very little taken away. Her collection of farmyard animals – articulated Edwardian donkeys and Tyrolean goats dwarfing the neat lead models – still crowded the shelves of a glazed corner cabinet above her head. A bunch of faded rosettes dangled from the key, teenage rewards to her and Mirabel for escorting Mr Fitzgerald's show lambs around the ring at the Bath and West. There was a wardrobe, its white paint chipped at the corners, and a big bow-fronted chest of drawers with several handles missing. Cherished relics were piled almost to the ceiling on top of the wardrobe, the layers settling with time into a solid mass of memories. Arbitrary fragments of the whole, like an open excavation.

Somewhere near the bottom, unseen but known by Ruth always to be there, was a folding child's chair from which, in a sense, she was still inseparable. Barely able to balance her own weight on bowed baby legs she had dragged the chair behind her wherever she went, grunting and muttering, screaming if her mother tried to part her from this precious emblem of . . . of precisely what she no longer knew, but the feelings she could recall better than yesterday's. 'I need it Mummy! I need it!' she had explained, as soon as she could talk. In her memories the chair was always there, and she was always sitting on it. It was on the floor of the library van, beneath the counter from which Mum served pulp romance to the Hampshire villages; it was in the kitchen when Mum was baking cakes; it was beside Granny's bed when they visited her in the Home; it was on the banks of the canal, and she was fishing with Dad on Sunday mornings before church; she was still sitting on it in the aisle of the church, a speck of dust before the altar of the Lord.

The handle of a miniature cricket bat poked out of the debris – her tenth birthday present from Mark, the clearest message of love he had ever given. Printed on the blade were the facsimile signatures of the Australian touring side they had seen play at Taunton that summer. From Christmas four or five years later, another present: Conor's pristine box of sandalwood soap. Her postcard albums. A tinplate model of the Eiffel Tower. Fragments of a palm branch, its dried-up leaves held together by interwoven strands of wool and tinsel – a skeleton of vanished pride, all that remained of the banner she had carried in the Easter parade at Wells a few weeks before her collapse.

A long cardboard box marked this division in the strata, the corners reinforced by rusty metal clips. Inside, folded by the unnamed tailor's hands between sheets of tissue paper, was a woman's black hunting coat, two white silk stocks, an embroidered waistcoat, and a pair of riding breeches: the present Dad had ordered in advance for passing the A levels she never took. Ruth had often considered taking the box down and looking inside, but dreaded what she might find – a shapeless mound of motheaten cloth, a dead litter of embryo mice? Or, worst of all, Dad's ambition for her, lying there in a perfect state of preservation.

Jumbled indiscriminately above the box were books, papers, photographs and diaries from more recent periods. The corner of a frame protruded: the petit-point panel from Dr Cardy's consulting rooms, an enforced gift, so dire had seemed her need for it at the time. For many years it had lived on the wall above her bed in the place where her own 'The Martyr's Gate' now hung, the painting she was most often sure expressed the truth. Somewhere up there on top of the wardrobe was a PVC beachbag containing the ninety-four shells and two starfish she had collected on the only foreign holiday her mother and she had managed to take since Dad's death, a visit to her godfather, 'Uncle' Gordon, in the South of France. Sylvia's wedding bouquet was there as well. There too, squashed into the corner, several of its wire bars sprung and the ring on the top long since lost, was her budgerigar's cage. Inside the cage, tightly tied with string, were bundles of letters – Dad's love letters which night after night she had been forced to read out loud to her inconsolable mother.

The day Dad died Ruth had fastened a black ribbon to his photograph on the wall above the chest of drawers; drooping and dust-laden, the ribbon was still in place. It was a hand-coloured graduation portrait taken by the college photographer in Bristol, three-quarter length against the backdrop of Clifton Suspension Bridge. Turning her head on the pillow, Ruth stared at Dad. For all its garishness, and despite the rigorous formality of the pose – right hand clasping left wrist, mortar-board to the thigh – Ruth adored this photograph. It was Dad before she was born, before he had met Mum even, and as he had remained for the whole of his dear life. Eyes bright with flawless conviction.

Eight years dead and he still protects us, thank God. With God.

The weight of exhaustion pressing Ruth's head into the pillow lifted, and she laughed.

How do we manage without Dad? We don't! He's here. He's always here.

He knew he was dying, though he never said. All those long talks. He was preparing us for the future, telling us the way he wanted everything to happen. The way he would have made it happen. I haven't forgotten a word, Dad. I haven't, you know. You know I haven't.

Mum's alright. I love her completely. And she looks after me all the time. We've done what you told us.

I'll finish my masterpiece. As soon as I'm better. You'll see.

And then? What then? I wish I knew.

I can't see any further. There's only darkness.

Today I'm not afraid of the darkness. I must pass through it, I know. He that follows the word of the Lord shall not walk in darkness, but shall have the light of life. I know.

There was a bang at the door and a rattle of crockery. Mrs Harrison had been listening out all morning for signs of life – she heaved her bottom against the door again, elbowing the latch, and backed in bearing a full tray of breakfast.

'You've missed lunch. Sylvia's washing up!'

They both laughed. Ruth sat up in bed and began to eat.

'Cereal first, silly.'

Mrs Harrison busied herself tidying away her daughter's clothes, scuffling about after a pair of vagrant shoe-trees and tossing the patent leather bootees into the bottom of the wardrobe. Whilst her grey hair retained some of yesterday's cultivation, she was back in one of her printed housecoats, the material badly worn where her stomach stuck out below the belt, and with faded patches under the arms. She sat down at the side of the bed and watched Ruth mop up the bacon fat with a corner of bread.

'What a day! How're you feeling? Those children're driving me mad. Can't they come up to you? Mark's off to play tennis at the Pembertons. Mirabel rang . . . Someone said – it was Mrs C, I think, though how she'd know I've no idea – that Mirabel's going to adopt. Did she say anything to you about adopting? It must be him. Can't imagine Mirabel having trouble making babies.'

Ruth lifted her mother's hands from the patchwork quilt and kissed the swollen knuckles.

'I'm so tired, Mum. So tired.'

'Of course you are, darling. What do you expect? You're not strong enough for all that gadding about. Not yet.'

'No? My poor old body. I'll just have to rest again.'

'A couple of days in bed and there'll be no stopping you.'

They looked at each other. And smiled. It was true what people said: having each other, and the times alone together at the Priory, made up for everything.

Mrs Harrison removed the tray from Ruth's lap and carried it off downstairs. When she returned a few minutes later for the chamber pot Ruth was asleep; she tweaked Ruth's nose to stop her snoring.

During the afternoon Reverend Hibbs called in on his bicycle to ask after Ruth, and on Mum's insistence stayed for tea. Though far down her list of candidates for a son-in-law, Mrs Harrison looked upon the mild middle-aged Lance Gibbs as a useful long-stop, and she was annoyed, for once, when Ruth refused to see the vicar.

'Not today, Mum. I can't today.'

'No? I'll tell him you're asleep, shall I?'

'Perhaps that's best. It's so kind of him to think of me. Everyone's so kind to me.'

She started to cry, silently, her large mouth stretched open. Her mother waited. Ruth rolled over onto her tummy and pressed her head into the pillow; she began to wail and beat her feet beneath the blankets.

'I want to speak to Mark,' she suddenly said, quite clearly through the pillow.

'He's not back yet, dear.'

'When he is he must come and see me.'

'I'll tell him,' her mother promised, and left the room.

Ruth turned round again and settled herself; her dark eyes, instantly dry, were fixed at a distant spot in the sky.

Shortly after six Mark was standing outside the door of his sister's bedroom. He knocked.

'Mark?'

He lifted the latch, and went in. Ruth had combed her hair and was sitting up in bed wearing a crocheted bed-jacket with a pink ribbon at the neck. Mismatched patches of rouge decorated her cheeks.

'Alright for some!' he said, taking up his customary position propped against the chest of drawers, his back to Dad's photograph. '*I've* been belting around in the sun all afternoon.'

Ruth felt he was pleased with her. She hoped so. There was something she needed him to understand.

'Did you win?' she asked.

'Did you play well you're meant to ask. In case I lost.'

'But you never lose, Marky.'

'Why ask then? Since you always know everything,' he replied crossly.

Oh Mark, Mark, why so angry?

'Because I'm proud of you.'

That forced a smile from him.

'I've got something to tell you, actually,' he said. 'We're having another baby. It's due in December.'

Ruth clapped her hands in the air.

'Mark! How wonderful!'

Careful. Not so loud. I mustn't get too excited. Mustn't get upset. He hates it so.

'It'll be a boy this time. I feel it in my heart,' she continued, in a calmer voice.

'I hope you're right. Dad would've liked a grandson,' Mark admitted.

'You'll call him Matthew, won't you? Of course you will. Matthew Mark Harrison-Sayers.'

Mark stroked his blonde moustache. He was fair-haired and lightly freckled, like his mother.

'You know, when he was alive I couldn't imagine living anywhere else but here. Even after he died. I was going to marry Mirabel and have three sons. Like the Fitzgeralds. And they'd have had sons. The Harrisons of Kenton Priory. That's how it should've been. Instead of this.' His hands flapped feebly at his side. 'Mum should sell this place. It gets you down, Ruthie. Would me. And Mum's drinking herself into the grave.'

'That's not true! You mustn't say such things.'

'Yes it . . . No. I'm sorry. I mean . . .' he tried again.

'Yes?' she encouraged.

'I thought you were meant to be better,' he blurted out.

Ruth suppressed a smile. *Now* he would have to listen.

'I am better, much better, I promise. You mustn't worry about me, Marky. Mum and I have everything we need. The peace and quiet, it's been blissful. It nourishes my work. I want nothing more than to paint. I was over-tired yesterday. And I was late with my pills. That's all.'

She paused. Mark was watching her out of the corner of his eye.

'I'm at the mercy of this feeble body of mine, with all its odd chemical imbalances. That's the way God made me. In time, with prayer and patience, it'll come right. It gets closer all the time. Every year I'm stronger. Dr Cardy's worked miracles and when I'm thirty, he says, my metabolism will be more or less stabilised. In six weeks I'll be thirty, and can begin to take my place in the world outside. Slowly and carefully, so so carefully. And never like you, of course! Not in London! Here in Somerset, in a quiet way. Then Mum'll be able to rest. And *I'll* be looking after *her*!'

Ruth looked up at Mark, her pale, inflated face awash with hope. Mark tugged at his moustache, risking a smile.

'That's our girl,' he said, and let himself be hugged.

At the door Mark hesitated. Ruth smiled, releasing him, and turned again to the window.

I *will*. That's what I'll do. Live in-between.

Mum's not really there, she's more with me. We'll live together, in-between. Cushioning the pain.

It's the best I can do.

I can only do my best.

3

Standing at her bedroom window in the appeasing moonlight Ruth looked more like the person she might have been than the one she had become. The shadowy shape of a woman's body, protected and enhanced by the folds of an ankle-length night-robe, high breasts and maternal hips; her face too, smoothed out and simplified, the female counterpart of her father's. It was late and silent, the time at which Ruth felt most peacefully part of the world.

The summer air was breathless. Through the still leaves of the poplars Ruth imagined she caught a glint of moonlight from the bow-waves of an impatient coot on the waters of Dad's lake. It would soon be dawn.

A sense of relief entered her body, a pin-prick, a tiny bubble burst, spreading balm through flesh and blood to the extreme nerve ends. Relief in the mind also, the relief of knowing she had done the right thing. This was how it had to be: it could be no different. Once it might have worked, many years ago, before the illness. Then she had dreamed often enough of how it was going to be. Even afterwards, when Dad died and she had found from somewhere the strength to nurse Mum through the devastation, again she had revived the dreams, relived the possibilities of youth. Now they were only memories; and rightly so. Conor had finally married someone else. And she was pleased. With me, dear Conor, you could not have borne the sadness. For me you would have suffered. For her you will be happy.

Now that Conor was married Ruth felt she no longer need resist the force of her love for him. Comfort lay now not in denial but in confirmation. His happiness was her fulfilment, and he *was* happy, and always would be, God willing. Years ago she had released him from his bond, had tried to exchange their adolescent love for friendship. It had not been easy. He had not wanted to go and she had not wanted to let him go. His belief in her had been so strong. Too strong. He had wanted more for her than she had wanted for herself. At first there had been nowhere to hide – not until she had started painting and could take refuge in the discipline of work. In the end Conor had been forced to give up, to believe her when she said she would never be able to marry. At the time she had decided not to tell him why, not the real reason anyway. It was better for him not to know. He was happy. That was the important thing. And the responsibility for his happiness was not hers. That was the most important thing.

I love you Conor. I love you too much to let you be with me. Seeing my failure reflected day by day in your loving eyes would have killed me.

Ruth closed the curtains and slipped back into bed. At seven-thirty she was woken by the Mickey Mouse alarm clock on the chest of drawers. Letting the bell ring itself into oblivion Ruth rolled out of bed and squatted sleepily on the chamber pot. The heavy release of blood took her by surprise. It almost always came when she least expected it. When she had given up waiting. She smiled: Mum would be pleased.

On Ruth's last trip to London to see Dr Cardy she had learnt that they now believed her kind of illness, the chemical imbalance everyone talked so much about, had a good deal to do with being a woman. Not simply with *being*, he had said, but with *becoming* a woman. Ruth tried to understand exactly what Dr Cardy had meant by this; and what it meant to her.

It was the suddenness of the original onslaught which she still found most terrifying. Even when she was feeling strong a fear haunted her, enveloped her, a fear that at any moment she might be struck down from behind, scythed to the ground and left again till bled of hope. To have once been relatively sure of some reward and to have been reduced, almost overnight it seemed in memory, to the certainty of nothing; to less than nothing – there was *not anything*, never had been, never would be. You can try to turn your back on such memories, can conceal them from others, can act as if they are not there. But they always are there really, and you know that, and dare not try to forget it. You dare not forget because for nearly eighteen years you lived a life of ease and joy, ignorant of the emptiness within you, of the something you lacked and everyone else possessed, of the something without which life itself could barely exist. You went on and on, year after year, never dreaming there might be anything seriously wrong – on the contrary, believing that everything was more right for you than for most – on and on and on. Until in a light-headed moment of overwork you left yourself behind and looking back saw that you were not there, and looking ahead saw you would never be there either.

And now Dr Cardy seemed to be suggesting that as a child she had in fact lacked nothing, that life really had been as it appeared to be. What was missing was some essential ingredient required only for becoming a woman, not for being a girl, an ingredient which her metabolism had been unable to manufacture in the normal way at the appropriate time. Dr Cardy could not tell her why her body had failed at such a crucial stage in her physical development, indeed he warned her to allow for a continuing margin of error in the drugs he supplied to redress the 'chemical imbalance'. There was no such thing as a complete cure for a condition such as hers; all he had promised was that she was getting better, much much better. In the passage of time, and with the cumulative benefit of her new pills, she had every right to expect one day safely to enter the realm of womanhood. Now that she was almost thirty it was right, Dr Cardy said, that she should think of playing a more responsible role within the family and in the community at large. Mum would not be able to look after her forever, and while Mum could still help and teach her it was important to learn to look after herself. You have been very ill, Ruth, she remembered him saying, word for word, more or less. You are still vulnerable and must move with caution, but believe me when I say, as I have said to you many times before, there is nothing inherently wrong with you.

Yes, I believe you. I do believe you. I'll get better now. I know I will. It'll take time because I've tired myself out with worrying about Conor. There's no reason for me to be like this any more. I'm not going to let it happen again. I'm not. You'll see. You'll all see.

During these days of slow recovery Ruth further refined her interpretation of Dr Cardy's diagnosis until she and Mum had again convinced themselves that everything, in the end, was going to be alright, that it was all somehow for the best. She slept much of the time, weakened by her period, the first for two and a half months, and mentally exhausted by the anguish of the previous week. As usual after such an attack, Ruth insisted on recommencing her morning and evening dose of lithium. Slowly and painfully, following the established pattern of recovery which they all knew so well, life at the Priory re-asserted its odd ungainly balance.

The warm wedding weather had continued on into July, promising a golden summer. Day by day the air in the studio became hotter and heavier as the sun rose in the sky, crossed over the top of the sharply angled slate roof, and sank down behind the trees at the other side of the house. The air trapped in the large room could never become too hot or too heavy though, not for Ruth. She loved to open the door of her studio first thing in the morning and feel the weight of yesterday's warmth against her cheek, to breathe in luxuriously the fragrant trails not just of yesterday but of the day before yesterday and of the day before the day before yesterday, of the seemingly endless days before that already distant day. She found waiting there in the morning the scent of pigments long since dry and covered over by later brushstrokes, of wallflowers already buried in the compost heap, of eaten oranges, and the lingering essence of Twinkle and Gabriel. Ruth seldom opened the windows while she worked, and at night, when she remembered, she closed the velvet curtains across the verandah to shut in the precious air. Suffusing and surpassing all the many other separate scents were aromatic fumes from the studio's cedar beams, balustrade and floorboards; during the day Ruth listened with pleasure to the old timbers creak and sigh, setting free the ghosts of winter.

Ruth's first action on returning to work was to push the two easels supporting her big picture into the far corner of the room, beside the grand piano. Her cross – her masterpiece – remained veiled. The piano also lay in shrouds, protected by a fitted blanket and covered with bunches of dried flowers her mother no longer bothered to place around the house. The flowers had shape but no distinguishing colours: blousy hydrangeas, spiky thistles, tight carnations were all a uniform dusty brown, like a gargantuan boxwood relief lying on its back across the top of the piano. The bulrushes had been separately sorted and set out in ranks along the full length of the covered keyboard. The last person to play the piano had been Dad himself, two evenings before he died. He had managed somehow to make it downstairs on his own – Ruth was at her desk but he did not seem to notice her and shuffled straight to the piano – all he ever played were three Mozart sonatas, and these he battled through one after the other without a mistake. When he reached the final chord tears began to fall onto the yellow keys down his emaciated cheekbones. He closed the lid softly and, without turning round, summoned his daughter.

'We must cover the piano, Ruth.'

'Yes, Dad,' she had replied.

At a certain time of day this corner of the studio was dappled in reds and blues from the outer ring of stained glass in the oriel window above the gallery; with passing clouds or wind in the branches of the trees, the colours flickered across the white muslin screen of the big picture like soft-focus lantern slides. Ruth did not need to lift the veil and look beneath. She could see in her mind's eye every brushstroke, finished and unfinished. Three years distilled into one picture. Longer. A lifetime. Past, present, and future. She was in no hurry to reach the end.

On first getting up from her sickbed Ruth felt too weak to spend more than two or three hours a day in the studio, and most of this time she sat with her feet up on the horsehair chaise longue, reading, the Bible mainly, and Elizabeth Barrett Browning's *Sonnets from the Portuguese*. Twinkle and Gabriel called in to see her every other morning and in Ruth's second week, the third after the wedding, she started a detailed red chalk portrait of them. Mother and child on the steps of the minstrel's gallery playing with a cracked Canton bowl of pebbles: 'After Leonardo' Ruth called her drawing, collapsing into helpless peals of laughter every time she made the joke.

'What's so funny?' Twinkle asked.

'Everything,' was the reply.

Her internal rhythms being so erratic, Ruth found it difficult to re-establish a decent daily pattern of work. Her delicate style of painting required a sureness of touch only achievable, she found, through disciplined labour; she first needed to feel in complete control, to feel so confident of her technique that the tip of each sable brush might reach out unimpeded from the depths of her heart. She adored the intensity of her painstakingly slow and, in some ways, simplistic method of painting. In all her work before the big picture she had also found otherwise unattainable satisfaction in channelling the passionate strength of her feelings into the everyday ordinariness of her subject matter. She still loved those little pictures of hers. They were much more than mere still-lives. Everyone said so. More, yes, but not too much more, not more than they and she could stand. Not like almost everything else in Ruth's life which buckled beneath the burden of her emotions. Only in the big picture, 'Thy Kingdom Come', had she managed to unite feeling and form in an acceptable manner. Ruth did not wish to enter the final phase of work on this until certain she was ready to paint at her best: as a test piece, a curtain-raiser, she looked around for the bones of another still-life.

Ruth was never sure what she wanted to paint until she began to collect together possible material in a haphazard fashion. This time, as soon as the decision was made to start, her eye alighted on a pile of magazines on one of the leather-fringed shelves of the bookcase in her studio: old copies of the *National Geographic*, their yellow spines cracked and torn from earlier tours of duty in the downstairs cloakroom. Ruth pushed a chair against the tall bookcase and clambered onto the lower cornice. She stood awkwardly on her fat legs, not daring to stretch fully upright as she reached blindly to knock half a dozen copies down onto the floor. They landed badly on the worn Turkoman rug, the covers of two torn away and the back of another broken, spilling its innards across the studio floor. Ruth picked up the pieces and put them on the chaise longue, the first applicants for a place in her new still-life. A sheaf of pigeon, pheasant and goose feathers stood in a preserve jar on the mantelpiece and she fetched this over to join the *National Geographics*.

Suddenly Ruth remembered the Christmas pine cones and dived amongst the debris beneath the gallery, eventually locating a cardboard box over the sides of which dangled tinsel, and home-made paper chains. She burrowed into the box like a terrier at a foxhole, fairy lights and streamers, all kinds of Christmas decorations cascading onto the floor where she knelt. She gave an excited cry and a moment later held up in the air two handfuls of pine cones, magnificent big ones, several glitter-sprayed in silver and gold. Winter: that would be her theme. Winter evenings . . . long winter evenings after high-tea when she struggled with her extra homework in Dad's study, Mum sitting by the fire listening to the radio through black bakelite headphones so as not to disturb. Both of them awaiting Dad's return: Ruth praying that her bedtime could be delayed till she heard the wheels of his car outside on the gravel. On certain nights, when the wind dropped and the old fir-trees ceased their muttering, she heard the Rover's engine rev as Dad slowed down and turned in between the eyebrows. On such nights she would jump up, fly downstairs, pull back the stiff hall door, and wait beneath the lantern in the cold. Through the open stone tracery of the covered porch she watched Dad's headlamps dance dizzily past the trunks of the trees as he descended the drive. It was too dark to see the car itself, just two yellowish beams of light bobbing along, guiding her father home. As he rounded the final corner and the headlamps arced across the flintstone façade Ruth waved, and sometimes called out – perhaps he could not see her?

Dad never altered course but continued down by the side of the house and in at the back yard. He once, only once, acknowledged her welcoming wave with a blast on the horn.

Dead leaves were what she now needed for her picture, fifteen to twenty perfectly preserved dead leaves. Ruth opened the French windows; it was a close day, threatening rain, and she wandered wearily across the tufty grass towards the spinney. At the side of the path leading to the stile she was surprised to come upon three miraculous leaves, gossamer hearts on sticks, transparent memories of summer glory. Ruth looked up to see what tree could have shed such magic on her untouched canvas. A leggy pine, with a ladder of broken branches leading to its mangy head, stood beside a sycamore in full, boorish leaf: neither of these surely, nor the two elms nearby, and certainly none of the scruffy elders which numerically dominated the spinney. She knelt down on the path and spread her cotton skirt to form a safe cradle for the three leaves, holding the hem of the skirt out in front as she struggled to her feet and walked towards the chestnut tree. Except for the ten beeches on the crown – which she placed in a category all on their own – this chestnut was her favourite tree. It looked so enormously heavy and earthbound from the outside, and yet inside, staring up through the bell-shaped body of branches, it seemed as light as anything. A puff of wind shivered the fishbone leaves and the chestnut tree appeared to hover above the ground, albeit firmly tethered by its roots to the fallen world. Ruth hunted about in the shade for the brightest brown leaves and laid them carefully in her skirt. She found one of last year's conkers too, its mahogany skin cracked and a maggoty tendril poking through. She licked the tendril with the tip of her tongue; it was warm to the touch and tasted sour.

Returning to the studio with a skirtful of leaves, Ruth made a detour past the monkey-puzzle tree and picked up a broken branch. She shook the branch in the air. It wheezed. Dust flew and wood-lice dropped onto the ground. She marched back towards the house with the monkey-puzzle branch held vertically in the air, like a sword, her gathered skirts exposing flabby white thighs. Mum banged on her bedroom window and waved. Ruth broke into a trot, pulling at the bunched hem of her skirt as though it were the reins of a horse, her mouth wide open, neighing, eyes fixed on her mother's.

The leaves, the branch and the conker she dumped on the floor beside the chaise longue. Ruth stood still for a moment, looking down at the mess on the floor, absentmindedly pinching the lobe of her ear. Bones on which she would paint flesh, reversing in her work the process of nature. She pinched harder, until her finger and thumb were numb, feeling neither pain nor pleasure. In *Sexual Manners* it said the man should nibble the woman's ear in order to 'facilitate the release of vaginal juices'. How could that work if there was no feeling at all in your ear? And what about those African women whose wood-wedged ears hung down to their shoulders? Ruth opened a drawer of her bureau and lifted out the manual, wrapped in brown paper. She flicked through the familiar diagrams – was it all a joke, perhaps? Ruth shoved the book back beneath its camouflage of used sketchpads, and went out to fetch some snails.

She turned right out of the French windows, each step on the diamond flags sending the poplar fluff and seeds of willow-herb swirling about her ankles, caught on the sheltered verandah like sand by a breakwater. The red brick of the garden wall descended in a sharp curve from the side of the house, protected for the first few feet at the top by terracotta tiles. The wall bulged dangerously, its crumbling cement supporting and supported by assorted weeds and mosses. Ruth kicked the wooden door hard, twice. It shuddered wide enough open for her to squeeze through, brushing against the branches of a pear tree. Half way down on the left a tall beech hedge separated Dad's rose parterre from the kitchen garden beyond. Box hedges flanked the crazy-paved paths laid out in the shape of a union jack. Amidst the rampant chaos Mrs Harrison managed to prune the smaller roses most years, but a pergola at the central crossing of the paths defied her occasional attempts at discipline and launched rose trailers rocketing into the sky, five or six of which had already landed in the middle of the parterre and re-rooted themselves. Inside the pergola, on a carved limestone column, stood a statue of Mercury, nude except for a large fig-leaf. Eight rustic seats lined the internal circumference of the pergola facing the statue, brick steps descending like a miniature amphitheatre to the base of the column. All the paths of the parterre, the whole garden in fact, sloped imperceptibly towards Mercury's bower. Damp and cool even at the height of summer, it had become a snails' paradise.

At her second step inside the pergola Ruth felt a snail's shell crush beneath the sole of her sandalled foot. Four others suffered a similar fate before she reached the other side, and walked over to the ruined greenhouse to fetch an empty flower pot, substitute bucket for the collecting of still-life snails. She crouched down amongst the ferns and dock leaves and pulled the snails roughly from the bricks, tossing them any-old-how into the flower pot. It seemed not so long ago that she and Mark had collected bucketsful of snails, set them out a foot apart on the back yard and crushed them on their pogo-sticks. Forty-four snails was the most they had managed in a single go. She remembered other victims of their childhood cruelty: daddy-long-legs sunning themselves on the fence by the sheep dip, their wings beating the air in vain as they tried to escape. Mark used to catch them by the wings and pull off all their legs, then one wing; he left the helpless bodies on the fence from which they floated to the ground. Ruth remembered the excitement of waiting for the ants to arrive, working in pairs to drag away the wriggling membranes of daddy-no-legs.

Ruth got up. Walking down the diagonal path towards the door she stopped abruptly, put down the pot of snails, and took off her knickers, wet through from sitting on the damp steps. She rubbed her bottom, drying herself with her skirt and continued down the path, knickers abandoned at one side.

It was then that a rustling of dry leaves directed her gaze to the base of the beech hedge, and she screamed.

Could it be? Could it really be? Clutching the flower pot to her chest Ruth made straight for the sound, pushing past the rose bushes as though they did not exist, heedless of the thorns tearing red stripes in her bare legs. It was! It was! It was Robin's tortoise, sitting in the shadow of the beech hedge, one beady eye blinking beneath his shell.

'Where *have* you been hiding?'

The tortoise had grown during the missing years, and Ruth put down the pot of snails to free both hands.

She lifted it close to her face. The tortoise stretched her pantalooned legs and clawed the air, stuck out her neck then pulled it in again. Ruth laughed and tried to kiss her silly head. No one, not even Mum, could know how much finding the tortoise meant to her. She was not sure exactly what it meant herself, she simply knew for certain that it had great physical significance. It felt . . . it felt as though she had found alive inside herself something which had disappeared so long ago she had assumed it must be dead. Something so small, so young, so unformed she could not tell what it would become – but at least she could feel it there, alive again, ready one day to grow into a shape she might hope to recognise and comprehend. Standing beside the dividing hedge in Dad's walled garden, the enclosed valley air stacked above her head heavy with thunder, she felt it inside her, outside her, everywhere. All over and all through her body. It was in the drops of sweat running down her spine onto the elastic waistband of her cotton skirt. It was in the blood throbbing in her ears. It was in the moistness of her loins, legs apart, open to the earth.

Ruth refused to believe in omens, in pagan signs or portents. In symbols, yes. Finding Robin's tortoise was a God-given symbol which, though it made no material difference, helped her understand herself. Now that the tortoise had come back it could go away again – once found no second loss could challenge her rediscovered faith in the events of that Christmas, when Uncle Gordon and Robin had arrived unexpectedly at the Priory, on Christmas Day itself, with lunch already on the table. It was the promise at that time of things to come which she had first ceased to trust and then discounted altogether, not the memories themselves. Such was the ferocity of Ruth's recall, the intensity of her love of loving, that for her it was not a matter of remembering the past but of being there. If Ruth could have seen herself at that moment in the overgrown rose garden, two weeks off her thirtieth birthday, knickerless, she would have sworn it was someone else. Oh no, that was not her at all – how could it be? Ruth was a young girl, recently rescued by her father from school. She had long hair hanging to her waist; and it was snowing.

'Good Lord. Gordon!' Dad exclaimed as he opened the front door.

Ruth had run to the door too, expecting it to be nice old Reverend Tolchard come for his Christmas lunch. She did not wait for her even nicer Uncle Gordon to reply but darted past the two grown-ups and grabbed Robin by the elbow.

'I got a pink tu-tu from Father Christmas. Want to see it? How's your tortoise these days?' she politely added, when the little boy refused to budge.

'Hungry I expect,' Robin replied. 'Tortoise is always hungry.'

Ruth folded her arms and crossed her legs, quite content to stand and chat on the mat if that was what the situation demanded.

'You could always call her Harriet. Like hungry Harriet the hatter's daughter.'

'Him! It's a him.'

The sex of Robin's tortoise was a bone of permanent contention between the two children, so much so that 'Tortoise' was the only name they could agree upon. Ruth made a funny face and shook her long hair from side to side, like the plume of a helmet, willing Robin to terminate the half-started quarrel. The boy had to smile in the end, and followed her into the Priory. Dad put an arm round Gordon Huntley's shoulders and ushered him in after the children. In the mock medieval hall a tree trunk smouldered in the open grate, fired by judiciously placed suckling logs. The two men warmed themselves and talked on while Ruth and Robin ran away into the music room where parcels marched across the floor from beneath the glittering Christmas tree. Mum looked cautiously round the dining room door, but was warned off by Dad's brisk signals behind Gordon's back: she could see that Gordon, her friend really, her first proper boyfriend in fact, was crying.

After the delayed lunch, and when the Queen had finished speaking on the radio, Ruth dragged everyone across to the music room for the present-opening ceremony. She had already sorted the parcels into individual piles and in a dramatic gesture divided her pile in two, one half for Robin who had brought no presents of his own. She made a deliberate division too, allocating to Robin the parcels which from much prodding and guessing and from past experience of the givers she thought he might enjoy; Mrs C's bumper Rowntree pack for instance; and Auntie Peachey's Beano Annual; even the large rectangular package from Dad, shopwrapped in Hamley's teddy-bear paper. (She knew for certain Dad's present was another family boardgame, and desperately hoped it was Cluedo – 'I accuse Professor Plum in the Ballroom with the Spanner'; or it might of course be Miss Scarlet, and conceivably Colonel Mustard with the Lead Piping – since playing Cluedo at the Fitzgeralds during Conor's half-term exeat it had become Ruth's favourite game.)

None of the adults attempted to explain to Ruth why Robin and Uncle Gordon had arrived, on their own and presentless, to cause this bustling upheaval to the Christmas regimen.

'Now there's absolutely nothing we can do today,' she had heard Dad say to Mum while he was making coffee in the kitchen. 'So just relax, will you. And leave it all to me.'

At twelve and a half Ruth felt older, much older, than her looks implied. Wiser too. Wiser than Mum in ways. It hadn't done them any good not telling her, had it? She knew now anyway, because it had happened; and still neither of them said anything about grown-up things. Their reticence, their failed protectiveness, gave Ruth a sense of power over her parents which she did not hesitate to exercise – even Dad had succumbed, acting against all his vaunted principles in fetching her home from Cadenham. She tested her power again on Christmas night, refusing to be parted from Robin.

'He'll be lonely on his own. Won't you, Rob?'

Robin obediently nodded his head.

'We want to stay together. In Granny's bed. With a bolster down the middle. Please, Mummy,' she pleaded. 'It *is* Christmas.'

Mum looked down at Robin, a thin child with transparently tender skin, and across at her daughter, the rounded rosy little creature whom everyone adored.

'Rascals! Come along then, let's get you washed.'

The so-called Granny's bed had nothing at all to do with either of Ruth's grandmothers. Granny Murray had passed away in her own very different bed, in a North London rest home, without once visiting the Priory; and Granny Harrison was a seldom-mentioned ghost who lived, and eventually died, in Hull. 'Granny's bed' was what it was called, not what it was: a tall, cast-brass bed with garlanded head-rest, sundry polished knobs, box mattress, maroon silk apron, and the softest, shiniest, deepest eiderdown Ruth imagined could ever exist.

'Are you asleep?' she asked, in a stage whisper, as soon as the lights had been turned out.

There was no reply.

'I'm glad you're here. *Really* glad,' Ruth continued. 'It's good you didn't go with your Mummy, isn't it?'

There was nothing much Robin could say to that either. He had already told her all there was to tell – about his mother and two older brothers hurriedly packing suitcases while his father was at church; about his helping them stow the presents in the car; and of how at the last moment he had slipped away with Tortoise and hidden in a wardrobe in the spare room. He had heard them shouting his name, but no one came to look for him.

Uncle Gordon's shock on returning from Christmas morning mass, and the frantic drive over from Bristol, Ruth could imagine well enough herself. She was not really asking questions but making statements, and doing the best she could to comfort.

'Tomorrow we'll make Tortoise a nest in the woodshed. Does she eat curly kale? Cows eat kale in the winter, you know, 'cos it's warmer than grass. I expect Tortoise'll like it once she gets used to it. That's what it's about *really*. Getting used to things. You can . . . Well, it's not easy, is it? I mean some things . . . some things you . . .'

Ruth was unable to finish her sentence. She had wanted to say that you can get used to anything if you try hard enough. It was the helpful kind of thing she had heard grown-ups say. Mrs Fitzgerald, especially: about her polio, and the fight to lead a normal life in spite of the irons on her leg. It was something Ruth would have liked to believe was true, but right then she could not do so. The thing which had happened to her that summer and continued to happen again every month, could she ever get used to that? And poor Robin. Not a single Christmas present of his own. His Mum running away. His Dad crying. How did you get used to *that*? Tears poured down Ruth's cheeks, and next to her in Granny's bed she heard Robin's choked-back sobs. Pushing aside the bolster Ruth wriggled across the cold gap in the bed and put her arms about her little friend. Instinctively he put his arms round her too and they pressed tightly together in the dark.

Ruth was first to wake in the morning. She listened out for sounds of movement in the rest of the house, wondering what time it was. She dropped cautiously to the floor at her side of the bed and tiptoed to the window. Low sunbeams lay dazzlingly bright across the snow – in two swift sweeps of the arm she threw back the curtains, and returned giggling to bed.

'Ooh, it's cold!' She shivered dramatically and made her teeth chatter. 'Hug me, Robin. I'm so co-o-old!'

Two small heads nose to nose on a single pillow, he with his arms around her neck, she with her hands clasped behind his back, they lay close and still. Robin smiled, and shut his eyes. Ruth tightened her hold: she felt warm and safe and loved, in a previously unknown way. She slipped down in the bed to press her burning cheeks against the boy's chest. With the woollen nightie rucked up around her waist she wrapped her legs about Robin's pyjamaed thigh, and squeezed. It was another world, a shared other world.

Ruth heard someone turn the handle of their bedroom door and, only just in time, pulled away to her side of the bed. Her heart beat erratically and she gazed in fear at her father's face, the steel heels of his shoes thudding into the linoleum as he walked towards her.

'Morning, children. Already awake? Good. Up we get then.'

Ruth frowned. Seventeen years? No, of course not. It couldn't possibly be Robin's tortoise. She replaced her – him, perhaps – at the base of the beech hedge, picked up the flower pot of snails, and walked slowly back towards the studio.

It was raining so hard next morning that Twinkle rang to cancel the portrait sitting. There being nothing else she could think of doing instead, Ruth set out her still-life on the square top of an oak side table and made the first mark on her waiting canvas, at the top right hand corner, an ivory crucifix, faithfully rendered in white tempera and near invisible. For a long time after this she sat on the art-school stool, feet resting on the worn top rail, hugging her knees and looking down at the snails. She saw the shells tremble and lift gently into the air as the horned head of each snail slid out of hiding. Eight snails had been selected for the painting and strategically placed on the yellow covers of four *National Geographics* which lay in an overlapping fan shape on a bed of brown leaves. The magazines were upside down – with the glass jar of feathers high on the left of the picture, five of the pine cones ranged across the top and the sprouting conker in the foreground – no monkey-puzzle branch. Ruth had decided on an almost vertical artist's viewpoint and was trying to fix in her mind precise borders to her complex perspective. Stretching down she moved the glass jar fractionally nearer the centre and adjusted the feathers, pushing the ends of some out of the picture space. She lifted a cock-pheasant's tail-feather from the jar and placed it flat across the magazines, contradicting the dominant direction of the composition.

'Huh!' she exclaimed, letting out breath. 'Got it.'

Ruth quickly gathered up the snails and put them back with their mates in the covered pot before they could escape amongst the leaves and ruin the carefully constructed patterns. Intending to leave the snails till much later, with firm slate-grey strokes of the brush Ruth outlined all the principal forms of the picture, finding the angles and creating the basic illusion of space without a moment's thought – confidently, naturally, as though the world was hers.

4

As the days of quiet recovery stretched into busy weeks, and as these weeks became months of successful labour at her easel, Ruth did begin to feel she might one day find her place in the outside world. There had been an important change; something important had changed. This time she felt sure it was all going to be different.

With the more feverish part of her occupied finishing off 'Thy Kingdom Come', the rest of her, the calmer part, had worked it all out, piece by piece. It must have happened gradually, this change, not suddenly: a long wide curve in the road which, at times, never seems to end, not a sharp corner. It must all have started, Ruth felt, when she dared commit to paper those first fuzzy images of the big picture, figures and forms from inside her private self which came to outside life beneath her hands; changed, matured and finally crystallised in the completed picture. Yet, very different though 'Thy Kingdom Come' was from her still-lives, Ruth acknowledged that the one would have been impossible without the others. And anyway, anyone looking seriously at those stricken dolls in her much earlier 'The Martyr's Gate', locked in to and out of love, was bound to see the same hand, the same mind, the same overwhelming passion at work. No, it was nothing so cut and dried as 'finding your true nature through creative expression'; Dr Cardy was wrong there. It had happened *while* painting, not through painting.

Now that 'Thy Kingdom Come' was over – lying veiled in a corner of the studio awaiting collection by the framer from Wells – the road had straightened out into a new landscape.

Sitting on her chaise longue in the weak November sunshine, both bars of a rusty electric fire warming her troublesome tummy, Ruth was unoccupied and unafraid. It was simple really, difficult but simple. A question of seeing yourself as you truly were. As God saw you, near enough – as near as you could without being God Himself. And without being afraid.

I'm middle-aged, almost, and running to fat. Must remember that. It's no use imagining I can take up life where I left it off, as if nothing had happened. Though, and Ruth laughed, it's funny actually: because that's the problem, isn't it? Nothing *has* happened, not to me, not inside. The world's older and my body's older, but I'm not. I'm still seventeen.

It's a shame. Still, there it is. God knows what's right. I leave it all to Him.

I suppose what'll happen is that all those years that I've missed, twelve, thirteen, whatever it is, will be squashed together and rolled up into the next six or seven, or so, before I'm too old to get married and have babies. There's such a lot I've got to do. Must look after my looks better for a start. Too many of Mrs C's cakes and crumbles, not enough exercise, that's my trouble. Every day from now on I'll spend a certain amount of time in the fresh air. All weathers. Go for long walks. Longer and longer, till I'm as fit as a . . . a fiddle?

Oh! Oh, Lord my God. My dear Goddi. You *must* look after me. Don't let me fail this time. This time I'm ready. Aren't I?

Ready and waiting.

It was the waiting, that was the problem; I never could stand the waiting. Perhaps I was too quick, too impatient, I don't know. I don't think so though. I felt ready, and was always made to wait: for everything. To go swimming on my own, to have riding lessons, for a ball gown, to wear a brassière. For summer, autumn, winter and spring. Always waiting. Certainly *not*, my girl, Dad used to say, there'll be plenty of time for all that when you're older. There wasn't, Dad. There isn't.

Of course it won't be the same now. You can't expect to be twenty when you're actually thirty. I'm not stupid! And I'm not going to be fussy. He doesn't have to be handsome and dashing, and certainly not young. So long as he's a true believer, in love and in God. That's all that matters.

Why shouldn't he be young and handsome too? I'm not *that*

bad. And when Mum dies I'll be quite rich. Mrs C says men prefer the mature type these days. Like me, she says.

We'll be two innocents discovering the beauty of love. My age will give him confidence. He won't be afraid because he'll assume I know; and he'll make love to me so passionately, with the purity of youth. And I'll respond with all my stored-up hopes and dreams, with a multitude of unkissed kisses, and he'll be mine forever. He'll come to me now soon and I'll take him in. I'm ready now. Now I'm ready.

Don't be angry with me. Be patient. Be gentle. Be loving. Be gentle. I'm yours, all yours. No one else's. Never have been, never will be. No one else's.

What can it be like? I know so little.

Does it hurt? It must hurt.

It hurt Cindy, Mark said so. He said there was nothing we could do because if we tried to pull them apart after they'd started we'd hurt Cindy terribly. She might even die, he said. There was nothing we could do. Just watch. Sitting on the grassy top of the ha-ha looking down on them at the foot of the wall. Cindy's high-pitched whine, nose in the air, her brown eyes staring up at Mark. Tongue hanging out. Trying to keep her balance while Jackman's sheepdog did his thing. Old Kim whimpered. It must have hurt him too. Stuck together, staggering about in the mud.

People can do it like that if they want to; it shows it in the book.

It *must* hurt.

A dog's thingummyjig's not soft, you know, not at all. It may look like a soft red worm. A warm, oily red worm which creeps out of its sheath and enters a girl dog when she's on heat – if they can get into the right position – makes babies and creeps back again. It isn't like that though, not like that at all. That red thing, his . . . his penis, a dog's cock, it's hard. As hard as a stick of rock. And sticky too. It *is*. I touched Joel's once, when he was lying in front of the fire in the dining room, and a bit of the red thing was sticking out. Very gently. He liked it. He licked my hand.

It's nice not to be afraid again. To be like I used to be: fearless of love – of making love. I'd make love all the time now, if I could. Make it and give it away as fast as I could. Nobody would run short of love with me around. Love thy neighbour as thyself. As myself? *Much* more. As much as my neighbour wants: touching; stroking; caressing; kissing; anything. You can do everything with love. Holding hands. Conor always wanted to hold hands. His big hand reaching for mine, the nails bitten to within millimetres of extinction. Between shots at croquet. Walking by the canal at Stratford on joint family outings. In the Pembertons' swimming pool. Holding hands, that's all he ever wanted to do. I kissed him once, though. No, twice. Once at that dance near Wincanton, and the other time . . . the other time was here, on the chaise longue, when Mark caught us.

They weren't proper kisses. He wouldn't open his mouth. Just rubbed his lips back and forwards across mine, quite fast; and held his breath; and closed his eyes.

Poor Conor. Afterwards, when I was ill, he wanted to kiss me quite badly. I couldn't though, I really couldn't; it was too late. I screamed and screamed.

If anyone else had tried I'd also have screamed. I would, you know.

I was too ill to be a woman.

Not any more.

No. It's different now.

I'm getting better, you see.

Ruth's thoughts, these forever unfinished conversations with herself, turned aside at that point to face the turtle-necked beau of Drill Hall dancing classes, Andrew Heath.

For years now she had trained herself to think of Andrew Heath as a complete stranger, as someone who had been around – there could be no denying that – but whom she had never known. In her memories she and he had never danced together, not ever, never touched, never exchanged a word nor even a glance. In her memories she knew nothing about him herself, only what she had been told by others. In her memories, where Ruth spent so much of her time, it always happened to someone else, more often than not to Mirabel.

Like the first time he touched her breasts. At the Simpsons' Christmas party. Downstairs in the Estate Office. The door locked. In the dark.

She was leaning against the filing cabinet, smiling, and Andrew Heath's hand was behind her back, undoing the zip of her blue dress. He pushed the stiff tailored sleeves down her arms and pulled the front of her dress to hang loose at her waist. He slid the silk straps of her slip off her shoulders and unclipped the hooks beneath the little pink bow at the centre of her half-cupped bra. It was cold in the Office and Mirabel's young breasts were ice hard in the moonlight. Andrew Heath's fingers stroked down and round and up again. She trembled. He bent his head towards her nipples, and she punched him quite hard on the nose with the palm of her hand.

'No, not yet, Andy. Not here,' she mumbled, and sat up, almost falling off the chaise longue.

Ruth threw back her head against the cushions and laughed out loud, pleased to have been caught out at last, to have slipped up and broken the self-made rules of her memory game. She pulled the tartan skirt up to her chin, spread her legs and put her hand inside her knickers. She was hot and wet, wide open. Hurriedly, clumsily, she kicked off her shoes and pushed the knickers down to her ankles. She fumbled with her distended clitoris, gasping for breath. She pushed and probed, feeling the walls of her vagina suck at her forefinger, feeling her forefinger press against the walls of her vagina. Ruth groaned, and lunged, again and again.

For several minutes she did not move, just lay there in the winter sunshine, brown woollen knickers dangling from one foot, one long white sock falling like a broken accordion around her ankle. Eventually she opened her eyes and reached with her free hand for a rag hanging on the stool. She wiped her crotch, her guilty fist, and the faded velvet of the chaise longue. Dropping to her knees, and hiding her face in her hands, Ruth burst into prayer. It was a confused, contrite prayer, pleading for forgiveness, for enlightenment and for the courage to make a new start.

Ruth pulled a cushion to the floor and moved closer to the electric fire, close enough to singe her sweater.

There was no harm in masturbating, Dr Cardy had said. Everyone did it, apparently; and not always on their own. Men did it to women as a preliminary to making love, he had told her, although she did not quite understand why. 'Of course it's perfectly possible to make very good love without vaginal penetration.' How? Ruth wished she'd asked him how. How do you know you've made love? She wished she'd asked him that too.

Ruth grimaced. There had been so many ugly scenes last time in hospital. She was much younger then. Nearly three years ago, now.

Dirty! Ukhhh, *dirty*!

Shaking her head aggressively from side to side, Ruth sent a fleck of saliva flying onto the hot fire. It hissed. She stared hard at the glowing coils; leaning forward, she fashioned a bomb of spittle with her tongue and let it fall from her lips. It landed on her knee.

'Missed,' she said out loud, and laughed.

It hadn't all been bad, though. There was Robin's first visit to remember. Poor old Robin. How worried he had looked. His taut cheeks blotched red with anxiety, his frightened eyes seeking hers across the intervening heads of other inmates. The embrace. The smell of his naval uniform, not of the sea but of the dry cleaner. The feel of his brass buttons pressing at her breast, and the surprising strength of his thin arms around her shoulders.

'There, there,' he had said, patting her hard on the back, trying to pull away.

Eventually she had let him go: 'I haven't got the hiccups, you know!'

They had laughed, like children.

Later, she had taken him out into the exercise yard to sit with her on a bench in the sun. He had let her hold his hand as he talked, telling her she must never give up, must never let herself become like the rest of them – the rest of the patients, he had meant. He had pleaded with her, begged her, not to forget the good times, had promised they would return. 'This is just a passing cloud,' Robin had said. 'Every silver lining has a cloud.' However lonely and afraid she felt, she must always remember how many people there were in the world who loved her: hundreds of people, according to Robin.

'Do *you* love me?' she had asked.

'Of course I do,' he had replied, contorting his face as if in pain. 'We all do.'

'When did you realise?'

'Realise what?'

'That you loved me.'

'Oh, I don't know,' he had said. 'Always have, probably.'

'I love you too.'

'Thank you.'

Had he squeezed her hand? Yes, Ruth still felt sure he had squeezed her hand.

'Will you come and see me again?'

'If you want me to. It's not too much of a strain?'

'A bit, but I don't mind you seeing me like this now. Not now that I know.'

'Know what?'

'That you love me.'

He had definitely *not* squeezed her hand that time. No, that was when he stood up.

'Would you be allowed out for a drive?'

'In your car? Like this?'

'Why not? If it's allowed.'

'Yes, yes. It's what Dr Cardy wants me to do.'

'Tea time tomorrow then?'

Ruth pressed her hands to her face, rocking backwards and forwards in front of the fire. It was easy enough now to see how wrong she had been. Of course Robin had not meant *that* kind of love. How could she have been so silly? Sitting in the car not uttering a word, seeing, hearing nothing, not moving, staring at him; at his hands on the wheel, his sinewy white hands; at his knees, at his thighs, at his crotch. Staring at his crotch, wondering where he was taking her and what it would be like. Ruth clambered up from her knees and sat on the edge of the chaise longue, hands still covering her face. Don't worry about that, she told herself, forget about all that. Remember his first visit. Remember it as it really was, full of affection. Be thankful for the kind of love you have, Mum's and Robin's and Conor's and Mirabel's and Twinkle's and Gabriel's; much more than you deserve. Ruth lay back on the chaise longue. Her eyes were open now, staring into future space, into a life without tension. It wasn't *inside* which mattered, it was what went on *outside* that she should be thinking about. Even if she did succeed in putting it all in order inside her head – and at times, at her easel, she had really felt she might be getting somewhere – even then there would always be the chaos outside to upset the balance.

You've first got to find your place in the story, one of the younger doctors had once said, before you can hope to make sense of the plot.

Time for a walk.

Throwing a coat carelessly over her shoulders, Ruth let herself out onto the verandah and turned towards the front drive.

5

On her first tentative steps into the outside world, Ruth wrote a letter to Mark offering to come up to Bradfield St Clare to look after the two elder children during the final week of Sylvia's confinement, and to stay on for as long as she was needed after the birth. It was a short letter, to the point, reassuring Mark that she was more in control of herself now than at any time since Dad's death, and telling him of her decision to give up painting. In a 'PS' she also gave her firm promise not to make a scene in front of the children.

When Ruth said she had given up painting she did not necessarily mean forever, only for the time being, till she found her feet. If she really was to make a clean break in the established ritual of her life, the 'paint-faint-paint' syndrome, as Twinkle called it, now was the time to do it, on the crest of 'Thy Kingdom Come'. With so much to learn, so much to experience in making up those missing years, Ruth could not afford to expend any part of her, as yet limited, resources merely painting – she needed all she had, and more, for the waiting world. As if to confirm the correctness of the decision, immediately it was made she felt the desire to paint dissolve and disappear, and then reform itself on the road ahead, in the far distance, like a golden locket dangled in the air, encouraging her with promises of future fulfilment; like a stick beating inside her head forcing her out into the open. She came to be convinced that it would be worth taking up the brush again only as a woman, a mature woman with no need to cheat her memory. Now that she could clearly see the possibility of future happiness there was no longer the same temptation to lie to herself about adolescent hopes and promises. Slowly, patiently, she would work now to recover as much of the lost ground as her damaged body could manage to hold on to. Step by step she would learn first how to look after herself and then how to look after her man, whichever man God gave her, whenever He decided she was ready.

Mrs Harrison disliked the idea of Ruth staying on her own with Mark, and said so: 'I really think it's best if I come too, darling. Just in case.'

They were in Dad's study in the tower, listening to 'Afternoon Theatre' – at least, Ruth was listening – to a play about a probation officer she had heard previewed the week before and was now having difficulty in understanding. Mum was playing cards, like a robot, turning and placing the cards on a baize-covered table she had set up beside her folding canvas chair, on the one spare square of carpet in the middle of the room. Ruth turned off the radio and rubbed her new John Lennon spectacles with the tails of her cardigan.

'I'll be alright, Mum. I'll take the train home the moment it becomes even a tiny bit too much for me. Promise.'

'Why go at all? You've been so well.'

'I *am* well. That's the point. I do wish you'd listen, Mum. I've told you dozens of times. I want to help.'

'Help Mark? What on earth for? I'd like to see the day *he* thinks of anyone but himself. There's plenty to do here if you want to help. Plenty. We could do the roses together this year. I'd love that. Make it all beautiful again. You'd like that too. You haven't started a new picture. Don't go, there's a dear. What's the point?'

Ruth got up from Dad's chair, pulling the tattered cover askew, and stepped across to her mother. She knelt at the side of the collapsible table and reached up to lay both hands against her mother's foundation-smeared cheeks. Mum put down the cards and squeezed Ruth's wrists.

'Are you listening this time?' Ruth asked.

'Yes, dear. Do tell me again. I'm listening.'

'I love you. I love you so much it hurts. I can . . .'

'I love you too,' her mother interrupted. 'But it doesn't hurt at all. Love can't actually hurt, it only feels like it does.'

'Mum! Will you please listen to me?'

Mrs Harrison giggled.

'Sorry,' she said, kissing one of Ruth's hands. 'Go on. I'm listening.'

'You know how I always used to pray that we'd die together? Remember? Well, I was thinking of you really. I was sure I was going to die first, and I didn't want to leave you here on your own. First Dad, then me. I couldn't bear the thought of your being sad about me dying too. Not so sad, I know. But pretty sad. And me not being here to love you better.

'Something has changed. Everything really. *I'm* going to live, you see, it's *you* who'll die. And I've somehow got to be ready for it.'

Ruth disengaged her hands which had been stroking her mother's cheeks, and clasped them together to form a cradle for her own head lying in her mother's lap. Mum's many-ringed fingers played with the rubber band securing Ruth's pony tail.

'Sometimes I think I must be mad,' Ruth continued. 'Imagining I could last a day without you. A second. How could I? I don't do a thing for myself. Sometimes I wonder if I could draw breath on my own. Without you being with me. At home. Just us two.'

'There's lots of life in the old girl yet!'

'Oh, I know, I know. God, I pray so. You've got to live to be ninety. A hundred. And I'm going to help you to. Don't you see? I'll be *your* life support.'

Ruth twisted her head in her mother's lap and looked up, wide-eyed and confident. Mum beamed back down at her.

'Lovely, dear. Can't wait. I'll become fat and bad-tempered, like my mother was. And you can serve me hand and foot. Push me along the drive in that old bath chair from the barn! Lovely. Start practising now if you like.'

The two women, so different in looks, one with grey-blonde hair and small bones, her face at times still beautiful, the other dark and big featured, launched into identical cackling laughs.

'When I get married we could make the studio into a nursery, couldn't we?'

'Yes, darling, whatever you want,' her mother replied.

Ruth had been to Bradfield St Clare only once previously, for the wedding weekend, when she and her mother had stayed with Sylvia's parents in the big house. 'One day this'll all be Mark's,' she remembered Major Sayers saying, with a sweep of the hand which had seemed to take in not just the house and the grounds but the whole of the village and half of Suffolk as well. Anticipating a fruitful marriage for their only daughter, the Major and Mrs Sayers had built a Queen Anne-style retirement residence for themselves in the main street of Bradfield St Clare, set back behind a line of plane trees and adjoining their principal farm buildings. It was into The Dower, as the new house was called, that Mark and Sylvia had moved; and it was there that they still lived, the promised exchange never having quite taken place. 'They're just running it in for us,' the Major still tried to explain, the excuse long obsolete.

It was all so very different from what Ruth had expected. Everything was so crisp and controlled: the sharp square rails of the front fence freshly creosoted; granules of grey fertiliser speckling the lawn; the red tarmac drive cleanly scrubbed, it seemed, cleaner than the kitchen floor at home.

'Is this it?' she double-checked with the taxi-driver. 'The Dower? Harrison-Sayers?'

'That's right,' the man confirmed, placing her bags beneath the porch.

'Wait! Wait!' she shouted as he began to drive away.

'Yes, Miss?'

Ruth ran round to the driver's side, waving a pound note in the air. 'But I haven't paid you. I forgot to pay you!'

'That's alright. On account.'

'Oh.'

Ruth remained standing in the middle of the drive facing her brother's home, its white windows smiling brightly. She smiled back, and waited for someone to open the door. She waited and listened, looked and listened for a sign of life. Where was the dog, the golden retriever Mark had told her about? Rufus he was called. She fumbled in her bag and pulled out Dad's silver pocket watch, removed from its customary place on the back of her easel. Three o'clock. Perhaps Sylvia had gone to fetch Pippa from school? Or perhaps Nanny Wimbush had, and Sylvia was upstairs resting? There was still no sound, except the clang of milk churns in a neighbouring yard. Can't stand here forever, Ruth told herself.

She walked across the drive and stood beneath the fluted columns of the narrow porch. There was an iron boot-jack on one side of the shiny black door and a bristling brush on the other, fixed to a pole. Instead of ringing the bell Ruth bent down to peer through the letter-box. The hall was small, its black and white diamond tiles continuing on through an open door into what looked like the kitchen. She let the letter-box bang shut, grabbed the brass handle, and pushed. The door opened. In she walked, across the hall and through into an enormous kitchen. She stopped again, and listened. Nothing stirred, all silent and spotless: polished pans hanging in neat rows above a crimson range; windsor chairs round a bleached table; a honey-oak dresser set with marked jars. Like a show house. Like walking into a brand new dolls' house.

There was a loaf of bread on the table, with three slices already cut, and a knife resting in amongst the crumbs. Ruth gave a sigh of relief, and put out her hand, dragging her fingers through the crumbs. Once this first sign of life at The Dower had entered her consciousness, others immediately appeared: a kettle simmering on the Aga; a doll lying on the floor; a clock chiming in the hall. And on the table, also, a note in Sylvia's bold hand: 'Ruthie. Gone to fetch Pippa. Back in twenty minutes. Make yourself at home. Love S.'

Those first two days were difficult for Ruth. She desperately wanted to help and yet everything she tried to do, even clearing the table after a meal, was finished off by someone else almost before she had started. At night, lying on the soft spare bed, listening to the muffled sounds of the television set in Sylvia's sitting room on the floor above, Ruth faced the certainty of imminent failure. Only Pippa's insistence on a good-night story and the taste of the child's darting kiss on her lips kept Ruth's hopes alive till breakfast, and on into another morning.

Whether it was she getting used to their pace or they to hers, whichever way round it was, Ruth had begun to find her feet by the third day. With an all-day daily help and the tireless devotion of Nanny Wimbush, there was actually very little Sylvia needed. Instead, Ruth made herself feel useful doing those jobs the others normally left till last. Like stacking the logs in the woodshed, or polishing rust spots out of the chrome mudguards of the pram. Things she could do in her own time, without the oppressive sense of being watched. One evening she designed a figurative nameplate for Pippa, and the next day painted it onto the child's bedroom door: the capital 'P' as a sleepy man-in-the-moon wearing a night-cap, the 'i' a candle held in the hand of a girl going to bed, dragging behind her a teddy bear, the other small 'p', the teddy in his turn leading a ladybird 'a'. It was a great success, not only with Pippa but also with Mrs Sayers, the latter's approval making Ruth feel much more relaxed. Having secured the support of Sylvia's fearsome Mama – 'the girl's not completely off her rocker after all' was the official judgement – Ruth found the Major also treated her differently, no longer holding in check his natural bonhomie. At lunchtime the next day, after Sylvia and her mother had departed in an ambulance for the Clinic, the Major took Ruth across for a drink at the Sun in Splendour, his daytime favourite of the three village pubs. Balanced on a bar stool, drinking Tio Pepe and sharing a joke with a group of total strangers, Ruth knew she had been right to leave home.

Accompanying the Major to the Burston Syndicate cocktail party at the Jockey Club was Ruth's first serious social test. One of the county's smartest annual gatherings, it was an event Mrs Sayers would have attended in glorious style, but for the imminent arrival of another grandchild (billed as the long-awaited male heir). There was no question, though, of Mark missing either the evening party or the day's great shoot at Burston Heath. 'Of course you'll go shooting, Mark,' Mrs Sayers ordered. 'Christ, it's Tankard day.' Before the War, with bags of over a thousand brace from the six prime drives across this force-fed tract of perfect sporting land, the Major had won the Tankard with a personal tally of four hundred and thirty-nine pheasant, twelve snipe and fourteen partridge. Nothing of this kind was possible any more, never would be again, and the Major had handed his gun over to his son-in-law. The Burston Syndicate was now better known for its socialising than its shooting, its exclusive invitations in gamebird brown-edged envelopes being keenly competed for.

'Are you sure you want to go?' Mark had asked Ruth the night before, the expression on his face making it clear what he thought of the idea.

'I don't know. The Major wants me to. Shouldn't I?'

'Up to you. Don't expect *me* to be responsible.'

Fearful of letting her brother down in public, Ruth tried to persuade the Major to leave her behind.

'I've nothing to wear,' she insisted.

'Yes, you have, old girl. The tweed suit. Mighty smart.'

'That? Oh, that's *ancient*,' she replied, blushing.

There was no escape, and in Mum's often altered pre-War two-piece, Ruth made an unglamorous, but not unsuitable, companion to the much-admired Major Sayers.

'Won't stay long,' he said as they walked across the raked gravel courtyard of the Jockey Club. 'Tip us the wink when you've had enough, there's a good girl. Don't want any accidents, do we?'

Amidst the noise of loud greetings in the chequered marble hall, and in her confusion at the provocative smartness of the women, many of whom displayed fresh Bermuda suntans and carelessly plunging necklines, it was several minutes before the news registered on Ruth. They all seemed to know what had happened, each and every one wishing to add their personal congratulations. Those who stopped long enough at the Major's side to be introduced to Ruth wrung her hand too before pushing on up the central staircase.

'Bloody good show, what?' she heard the Major say. 'Chip off the old block if ever there was.'

Ruth felt an infusion of panic and excitement flood the empty pit of her stomach, and she tugged at the pin-striped sleeve at her side.

'Is it, is it a b-b-boy?' she stuttered.

The Major raised both bushy grey eyebrows and regarded Ruth with what, in anyone but him, would have been interpreted as a look of fear. The eyebrows rocked and subsided, the eyes twinkled, and he chuckled to himself.

'No, no. You've got it wrong. It's Mark. He's won the Tankard. Always said he would. Best young gun I ever saw.'

For more than a moment, gripping the Major's arm with bruising intensity, her face white and blank, Ruth appeared on the point of disintegration. She blinked and shook her head, and the colour rushed back into her cheeks.

'How wonderful,' she said.

The Major took Ruth's hand and towed her in his wake through the milling crowd of would-be gentry.

'Where's he hiding? Bloody good show. Another Sayers on the mug.'

They found Mark in the Committee Room, still wearing his plus-fours as tradition demanded of the victor, surrounded by a flock of middle-aged sirens. The Major clapped both hands on Mark's shoulders and drew him into a soldierly embrace. Mark winced, and stepped back on release, knocking his heels against a leather-padded fender and almost falling over.

'Well done, Mark, old son. Great day for me. Dream come true. Thank you, my boy. Thank you.'

It was Mark's turn to blush, and his tongue licked the clipped fringes of his blonde moustache. Despite the pavlovian pulling away from physical contact, Mark could not have been more delighted. Glowing with the praise from his adored father-in-law, he laughed shyly, a light tumbling laugh.

'Lot of luck really,' he said. 'They flew right at me all day. D'you know, even in number seven butt on the Paxton Wood drive I got fifteen and a half brace dead overhead. Dead down my barrels all day long. Amazing. I'm pleased you're pleased, though.'

For once it was clear to Ruth that nothing was required of her, in fact that the less she said the better. Smiling continuously and catching Mark's eye as often as she could, Ruth stood peacefully in the Major's shadow. She spoke when spoken to, listened and watched, and held in front of her an untouched glass of champagne. Only at the victor's toast, a loudly hurrahed affair with the Major himself presenting the silver tankard to Mark, did Ruth take a sip from her glass and throw back her head to join in the bellowed bravos. Shortly afterwards the Major bid farewell to everyone, and drove her home to Bradfield St Clare.

With her mother away, little Pippa spent most of her out of school hours playing with Auntie Ruth. There seemed no end to the different games they enjoyed together: dressing-up games; mother and father games; where-in-the-world-would-you-want-to-live-if-it-was-not-here games; I spy with my little eye; Old Macdonald had a farm; I packed my bag for a holiday by the seaside and at the bottom of my bag I put a duck-billed platypus; once upon a time . . . When Sylvia returned home from hospital with baby James she found Ruth had changed so much in appearance as to be, not unrecognisable exactly, nor 'a different person' as Mrs Sayers put it, but a revelation. Even Mark was happy to admit it all seemed to be working out very much better than he had feared it might.

On the next Sunday Mark drove Ruth and Pippa over to Morning Song at Ely Cathedral, and on the way back they stopped to test the ice at Setton Lode. It was years since Ruth herself had last been skating, but she contented herself with helping Pippa into new white boots and watching the little girl skim off across the ice after her racing-skated father. Ruth slipped and scrambled up the giant-sized drain and walked along the top, the ice stretching below her in an unbroken line to Ely Isle. She saw Mark outstrip each imagined rival on the ice, turn sharply, and glide leisurely back towards the Christmas-red figure of Pippa. He picked her up and whirled her round and round till Ruth herself, half a mile behind, could hear the girl shriek: 'Stop! Daddy! Stop!' Ruth stood still, and smiled; it was amazing to think how little Mark had changed, how little anything changed, despite appearances.

On the way home Mark had a long conversation with Pippa whom he insisted sit on her own beside him in the front of the Range Rover.

'Is it nice having Auntie Ruth to stay?' he asked.

'No. Horrible,' Pippa replied, an over-excited, nearly six-year-old bouncing up and down on the seat.

Mark gave the child's leg a hardish slap.

'Don't be rude, Pip. Answer properly.'

Pippa leant her chin on the back of the seat and fixed her eyes on Ruth's as she replied: 'I love Auntie Ruth with all my heart.'

'You do, don't you. She should come and see us more often.'

Pippa had turned again to gaze ahead through the wind-screen.

'What's that, Daddy?'

'What?'

'That thing there. See?'

She was pointing at a grain silo.

'That's a place for storing the harvest.'

'Why?'

'To keep it dry.'

'Why?'

'Why do you think?'

Pippa thought for a moment.

'So it doesn't get wet. It was good skating, wasn't it, Daddy?' she went on, changing the subject.

'Mmmm. Next time you'll have to make Auntie Ruth skate too. She used to be very good. On our lake, beautiful figures of eight. And she never had lovely skates like yours. She wore some funny Swedish things strapped to her boots. They're probably still around somewhere.'

'Not given away by Granny? Like the rocking horse?'

Mark took one hand off the wheel and stroked his daughter's hair. 'No, not like the poor old rocking horse,' he replied.

'Why did she do it, Daddy? Why did Granny give away your rocking horse? Why?'

Mark snorted a sort of laugh.

'Oh, I don't know why. Does it matter? You've got a lovely rocking horse of your own now!'

'Ye-e-es, I have, 'strue,' the child said, not entirely satisfied, trying to work something out in her mind. 'But I'd die if he was taken away from me. I would. I'd die. In my sleep. Like the other Grandpa.'

Mark wondered how to respond to his daughter's confused emotions.

'Dobbin will never leave our house. When you're too big for him then Alice will ride him. And when Alice grows up too, then baby Jamie'll look after him. Then . . . then when you're big like Mummy and have a Pippa of your own you'll come and stay and Dobbin'll still be there. He'll always be at home with Mummy and Daddy. Always.'

He looked at Pippa out of the corner of his eye to see whether his explanation had been accepted: she was fiddling with the knobs of the radio, her rocking horse trouble forgotten. Mark glanced up at the rear-view mirror and found Ruth staring at him. Her dark eyes smiled encouragement; and he smiled back.

'Awful name, I know. I pushed for another Pegasus but Sylvia's mother got her way. Probably for the best. All in all.'

With a week to go to Christmas, Ruth was persuaded to change her plans and extend her visit into the New Year. Unable to control her dismay when Ruth telephoned with the news, Mrs Harrison nevertheless accepted the invitation to stay at the big house over the holiday period, promising to catch a train on the morning of Christmas Eve.

It was a busy week, on every evening a cocktail or dinner party, often both, to most of which Ruth was also asked along. Mindful of her past record and of the inherent precariousness of her progress, Ruth usually stayed at home. It seemed churlish though, childish even, to turn down all the Major's proposals; so now and again she joined the family outings.

The most disturbing thing about going to parties, Ruth found, was never being quite sure whether she had enjoyed herself or not, and if not why not. Wedged between Sylvia and her mother in the deep back seat of the Bentley, listening to the Sayers' post mortem on the party, Ruth's immediate after-feeling was often of joy at being out in the world and of relief at the meaninglessness of it all, delighting in the foolish way they laughed at others' foolish ways. It was clear to her that many of the things she worried about, like catching people's names when introduced, and not knowing anything about opera, actually did not matter at all. Ruth had never considered herself an expert on art, and yet when the Pre-Raphaelites came up in conversation at one of the parties, three of the ladies she was standing with had never heard of Holman-Hunt, and the hostess herself seemed uncertain who Raphael was (though according to the Major she was slightly drunk – 'pissed as a newt', Prudence Sayers confirmed). With practice Ruth duly convinced herself it was wrong to take things as seriously as she did, some things anyway. Some things in life just had to be accepted whether you understood them or not. Everyone else did. She did too, some of the time. Could she learn to do it all the time? Perhaps. It would be difficult though. Very, very difficult. Something, some silly thing always happened to set her thinking again. Worrying, panicking, longing to run back to the studio, to the in-between world. Her peace of mind was still so easily ambushed.

'Quite a nerve serving nothing but stale Twiglets,' Mrs Sayers was saying on the way back from the Hislops. 'Mean as two short planks!'

'Come off it. There were those delicious dips. From La Girondelle,' Sylvia insisted.

'Were there? Where? *I* never got a sniff of any.'

The Major, driving with caution across a patch of black ice, chuckled.

'What's so funny? And do we *have* to drive at this snail's pace? I'm starving.'

The Major guffawed and, by mistake, hooted the horn.

'What's so bloody funny?' his wife repeated.

'Joke. Not for a lady's ears I'm afraid, darling.'

'Try me.'

'No, no. It's too crude.'

'Can't be. Where did you hear it?'

'At the drinks actually. From Madge Hislop.'

'Madge? But she's a Catholic. Don't be a twerp. Of course you're going to tell us.'

He did tell the story, typical of its kind, all too graphically explicit for Ruth to miss the meaning.

Is this funny? Is it? They all laugh. Mark too.

It must be me.

Why, why do I have to take everything so seriously?

It was this sense of always being in the wrong, coupled with her determination to secure a foothold in the world as she found it, different in so many ways from how she imagined it to be, which prompted Ruth to accept William Baillache's invitation to dinner on the night before Christmas Eve. Mr Baillache, Will, as the Major suggested she call him, owned a stud farm over the other side of Ickworth Park, at Denham End. He was in his forties, and a bachelor. Ruth had met Will on several occasions, and admired his encyclopaedic knowledge of wild birds; she had also found him attractively inept at making conversation. The stud, inherited from his Uncle four years before, was reasonably successful – 'very second eleven, though', as Mrs Sayers would have it – and just about ran itself.

William Baillache was eminently available, had been all his life.

'Never been to La Girondelle before have you, R . . . er, Ru . . . Wooff?'

Will, who suffered from a chronic lisp on both his 'r's and his 'th's, made a terrible hash of her name, sounding like a child barking.

'No, I haven't. It's meant to be very nice.'

'So people say,' he replied, secure on his 's's. 'My first time too.'

Nothing more was said until they drew up at a thatched cottage on the outskirts of Bury, West Suffolk's newest and smartest restaurant. The table was booked for eight. They had arrived fifteen minutes early and a knuckle-cracking Spaniard with shiny white shirt and brown teeth insisted they retire to the inglenook and accept, compliments of the house, an aperitif of their choice.

'Awfully kind. What'll you have er, Ru . . . er, what?'

His painful shyness did not worry Ruth; on the contrary, it gave her confidence.

'I don't know any aperitifs. Why don't we have whatever he suggests. Nothing too strong, though,' she added, giving Will a conspiratorial wink designed to put him at ease.

When he dropped her back at The Dower after dinner, Ruth squeezed his hand – hard – and thanked him for a lovely evening.

'I enjoyed it myself,' he said. 'We must do it again.'

'Yes, we must. Goodnight, Will. Take care.'

Ruth stood in the porch, waiting till the car turned out through the five-bar gate into the High Street: she waved, and he waved back. What a nice, kind man. And he had really enjoyed himself, Ruth could see that.

Had she?

Oh yes, in ways. It had been nice watching him relax; and she had liked the sound of her own voice, for once.

But what else?

But, nothing. If she could do it there why not at home too? Where it mattered. There was no difference, really, between life in Watham and life in Bradfield St Clare. She had always imagined two worlds, hers and theirs, but that wasn't true, her world was theirs too, if she'd allow it to be. She could see that now.

The two worlds were the same, at the centre.

Not that it would be easy, after all these years, to live outside. But she would. She'd let the world into the Priory, into the studio even, and take the Priory out into the world.

Before going to bed Ruth sneaked into the kitchen to telephone Mum. 'Shhh! Don't shout, you'll wake Mark . . . I'm coming home . . . Yes, tomorrow . . . No, everything's fine. I just wanted to be with you . . . I know you are, but don't. I'm coming to you instead . . . I'll tell them, don't worry. They'll understand . . . Yes, I will. 'Bye. Love you . . . Me neither. Goodnight, Mum. 'Night.'

Ruth felt relatively calm and clear-headed. The stay at The Dower had succeeded beyond her furthest hopes, and could easily have continued. There was no longer any point, that was all, nothing personal. She felt only gratitude to them all, Mrs Sayers included – to her more than the others perhaps, since it was through her that she had seen the light, had discovered how glad she was to be herself. Different things mattered to different people. She felt she still had much to learn, but nothing to be ashamed of, not now. She simply wanted to go back home.

6

For the first time in many years, despite the crowded Christmas train journey earlier in the day, Ruth felt strong enough to wait up for midnight mass. Rushing into church, their regular three minutes late, Mrs Harrison and Ruth were ushered to a place at one end of the Fitzgerald family pew, the kneeling Fitzgeralds gladly squashing closer together, whispering 'Happy Christmas' down the line. Lance Hibbs hesitated in his sing-song recital of the Ten Commandments and nodded a welcome, before leading his flock on again through the ordained responses: 'Honour thy father and thy mother; that thy days may be long in the land which the Lord thy God giveth thee.' 'Lord, have mercy upon us, and incline our hearts to keep this law,' they replied . . . 'Thou shalt not covet thy neighbour's wife, nor his servant, nor his maid, nor his ox, nor his ass, nor any thing that is his.' 'Lord, have mercy upon us, and write these thy laws on our hearts, we beseech thee.'

Ruth stared ahead, eyes walking up the worn chancel steps and along the black, cream and terracotta tiles, climbing onto the altar itself and into the stained-glass arms of the risen Christ. Every word of the Collect, Epistle and Gospel she repeated to herself, glorying in their familiarity, and celebrating her intimacy with this holy place, a place she had looked upon as partly hers ever since her reception into the family of God.

She saw herself as she thought she then was, fifteen years before. Saw herself as, it seemed to her, she could be again.

'Defend, O Lord, this Thy Child with Thy heavenly grace, that she may continue Thine for ever; and daily increase in Thy

Holy Spirit more and more, until she comes unto Thy everlasting kingdom. Amen.'

That was what the Bishop had said at the laying on of hands in Wells Cathedral. One hand resting on her head, on her wavy black hair, the new white plastic band too tight, chafing the skin behind her ears. An old hand, with brown spots and swollen knuckles and a gigantic garnet signet ring. His other hand rested on Twinkle's pointed head, the top joint of one finger missing. The two school friends knelt side by side on the altar steps of Our Lady's Chapel, Miss Thin and Miss Thick, one light, one dark, the brightest pupils at Shepton High, first, always first in their respective years. Dad's Reverend Tolchard had been vicar at Eastney and Watham then and had guided the girls through ten months of fortnightly confirmation classes. A pair of angels he had called them, his angels of redemption.

Ruth loved the Gospel for Christmas Day, more than any other passage in the whole of the scriptures. She adored the roll of its language, the mnemonic beat of its verbal repetitions, and worshipped its mystic message: 'In the beginning was the Word, and the Word was with God, and the Word was God. The same was in the beginning with God.' She directly felt its awesome power, and was inspired: 'All things were made by Him; and without Him was not any thing made that was made.' She cherished the hope which quickly followed: 'In Him was life, and the life was the light of man.' Lightness and darkness, hers and His: 'The light shineth in darkness, and the darkness comprehended it not.' And at the end of the Christmas Gospel she wept in gratitude for her Lord's birthday promise of fulfilment: 'But as many as received Him, to them gave He power to become the sons of God, even to them that believe in His Name: which were born, not of blood, nor of the will of the flesh, nor of the will of man, but of God. And the Word was made flesh and dwelt among us, full of grace and truth.' Amen, she cried. Amen. Amen. Amen.

Ruth recalled the years of darkness illuminated solely by her vision of Christ on the cross, by the beauty and brightness of his tortured body. She suffered as He suffered, surrounded by the unyielding blackness of the world outside, the blackness of incomprehension.

'And He shall come again to judge both the quick and the

dead; Whose kingdom shall have no end.' Ruth whispered the words of the Creed, a smile playing across her face as she turned towards the candlelit fir tree behind the lectern. Everything was changing. Slowly, imperceptibly a soft light was pushing its way through, casting shadows across the rocks, dark shadows but lighter than the tangible blackness of the past. She was excited and at the same time frightened. She had become so used to shuffling blindly along the old path, round and round in a circle, trusting the touch of familiar objects to guide her through from day to day. Used to making her way without haste from canvas to canvas, each completed still-life a post in the ground reminding her on successive circuits that she had been there before. Now that she had left the track, head up to sight the distant flickering shadows, would she ever find her way back? Would she ever want to? The bright light of truth could, she knew, be warm and comforting. It could also be cold, hard and merciless. The pleasure and pain of His naked truth.

'Therefore with Angels and Archangels, and with all the company of heaven, we laud and magnify Thy glorious Name; evermore praising Thee, and saying, Holy, holy, holy, Lord God of hosts, heaven and earth are full of Thy glory: Glory be to thee, O Lord most High.'

The Reverend Hibbs walked up to the altar and knelt down on one knee, hands and forehead resting on the white altar cloth. A young priest whom Ruth had not seen before fiddled at the side with the patens and chalices. The steel studs on the sole of Lance Gibbs' protruding shoe danced in reflected light from the midnight candles. Mrs Harrison nudged Ruth, and giggled, pointing at the rector's shoe.

'Grant us therefore, gracious Lord,' he was saying, on their behalf, 'so to eat the flesh of Thy dear Son Jesus Christ, and to drink His blood, that our sinful bodies may be made clean by His body, and our souls washed through His most precious blood, and that we may ever more dwell in Him, and He in us.'

'Amen,' came the congregation's reply, a many-headed growl of assent.

Ruth clasped her hands together as tight as she could, biting her thumbs as she tried to rid herself of all the unholy images tumbling through her mind. This, at least, was nothing new, the desire before taking the sacrament to dedicate herself in cleanliness and purity to the love of God, to empty her heart of all feelings other than for Him. Filing out from the front pew, Ruth was one of the first to the altar rails where she dropped heavily to her knees, still muttering, eyes screwed shut, chin on chest, one hand held out supported by the other.

'The body of our Lord Jesus Christ, which was given for thee, preserve thy body and soul unto everlasting life. Take and eat this in remembrance that Christ died for thee, and feed on Him in thy heart by faith with thanksgiving.'

Ruth felt the wafer of unleavened bread pressed into the palm of her hand by Reverend Hibbs. She lifted her hand and lowered her head, catching the sliver of holiness on her tongue and letting it melt in her mouth.

'The Blood of our Lord Jesus.'

Such a gentle voice: Ruth opened her eyes and saw the young priest bend away from Mirabel and approach her. He tilted her chin with the touch of his dry forefinger and let her lips rest for as long as she wished, it seemed, on the brimming chalice.

' . . . Drink this in remembrance that Christ's Blood was shed for thee, and be thankful.'

Be thankful. Of *course*, how could I ever have forgotten? It's not enough not to complain, I must actually be thankful. I am, oh I am, Goddi. I really am. And I've never blamed you, not for a moment, you know I haven't. I can only be who I am, and what you make me.

Ruth struggled to her feet and returned to her place. There were fifty, maybe seventy, people queuing for Communion, many of them strangers, Christmas guests in the neighbourhood. Twinkle was there too, Gabriel fast asleep in her arms, bigger than baby Jesus. She gave him to Ruth when her turn came to approach the altar.

I don't deserve it.

It doesn't matter, no one does. It's God's will. That's all there is to say. God's will. He puts Gabs here in my arms. And He takes him away. He makes me ill. And He makes me better. He's always here, and *that*'s what I must never forget to be thankful for. Never.

'The peace of God, which passeth all understanding, keep your hearts and minds in the knowledge and love of God, and of His Son Jesus Christ our Lord: and the blessing of God

Almighty, the Father, the Son and the Holy Ghost be amongst you and remain with you always.'

Early in the New Year, determined to fulfil her promises, Ruth joined Mrs Fitzgerald's amorphous band of Parish helpers.

'Marvellous, Ruthie. What a pity we didn't have you last month. Never mind, you can design the Lenten Address programme for Wells. I've got Lord Lytham this year. The Bishop's furious. Would you, dear?'

'If you want, yes. What else?'

'That's enough to be going on with. Don't want to interfere with your real work, do we?'

She leaned forward and patted Ruth's hand. They were in the morning room at Lee House, sitting either side of Mrs Fitzgerald's business-like partner's desk, the coffee percolator gurgling on a tin tray and puffing steam between them. Ruth held the older woman's lopsided gaze for several seconds, then lowered her eyes, feeling as she often did with Conor's mother that nothing could be hidden from her. That nothing should be.

'I've stopped painting,' she said. 'To have a baby.'

Mrs Fitzgerald was caught with the coffee cup half way to her lips; she frowned, and replaced the cup in its mismatched saucer.

'I'd no idea. How nice. Am I allowed to know who the father is?'

Ruth clamped her hand to her mouth and successfully stifled a hoot of laughter.

'No, no. I'd *like* to have a baby. I'm still . . .'

'Oh, I see. Sorry, I thought . . .'

It was Mrs Fitzgerald who started them off, letting out an ageless giggle. Ruth followed. They kept catching each other's eyes and beginning all over again, until Ruth's glasses steamed up and she could no longer see.

'I'll have to look for someone good enough, now I know you're on the market,' Mrs Fitzgerald concluded, before moving on to other things.

One of the duties allocated to Ruth at the next church committee meeting was co-ordinator of the graveyard restoration project. In coining the title 'restoration project' Mrs Fitzgerald and Lance Hibbs had cleverly elevated the unpopular task of keeping tidy the Parish's three graveyards into a fashionable issue of heritage preservation: numerous volunteers, who seldom bent a willing knee in their own gardens, fanatically weeded the graves of strangers. Being only a quarter of a mile down the road from the Priory, Watham Churchyard was of special concern to Ruth. It was here that Dad was buried, where Mum and she intended to follow, and since his death its grass verges had been cut and maintained at the Harrisons' expense by Mr Cornish and young Ted. Bringing in a team of helpers to tackle the wilder confines of this hallowed place appealed to Ruth as the perfect first act of her new communal life. On the last afternoon of that leap year February, as she and her team cut away the brambles from the long north wall of the churchyard, Ruth knew Dad was well pleased with her. She as good as felt his cold pat on her back.

The only disturbing feature of the work was the proximity into which it brought her with Ted Turnbull, 'young' Ted as he was originally called in deference to his father, now dead. Seeing young Ted now, a dour tractor driver from Lee Farm and the pious father of five teenage daughters, Ruth seriously wondered whether she might perhaps have imagined it all.

'Grand job, Miss Ruth,' Ted pronounced before going home for tea. 'Don't worry about clearing up now. I'll be down with the old trailer one day next week, no trouble.'

'Thank you,' she said, her face too hot from the afternoon's exertions to blush any redder.

He still walked the same way, long strides, hands in pockets. The same whistle too, a surprisingly tuneful, gap-toothed warble.

Fourteen years ago? Young Ted was already old enough even then to be married, and every year in the middle of November his frisky Welsh wife presented him with another baby girl. Three of them before he left the Priory for a better-paid job with the Fitzgeralds. They joked about young Ted in the village, but with respect. The fifth came on time again to the day, and Ruth could still remember something of Dad's excitement on hearing about it in the evening after work. Mum was very excited too, Ruth seemed to remember.

Ted's wife died before the sixth child was ready to be born. Died in bed, with Ted on top of her, according to the story. Finest ram in the flock, young Ted, so it was always said.

Yes?

But that was all much later, after Ruth's breakdown, at a period in her life where she found great cavernous gaps in her memory. Before her illness, though, what exactly had happened then? Surely she could remember that?

It was a 'crush', there was no denying it. Everyone else at school had crushes and it was a relief to have one of her own. All the same she did find it odd at first, and had to force herself into the established rituals, taking Cindy for endless walks around the garden and down to the lake, so she could see and be seen by young Ted. It soon enough became serious, and she bought herself a Woolworth make-up kit to keep behind the mirror in the greenhouse lavatory. Every teatime after school, decked out in lipstick and eye-liner and with white socks pulled up over her knees to look like stockings, she went in search of Ted.

'Afternoon, Miss Ruth,' he always said when she passed. 'Looks like rain, I'd say.'

Ruth swung Cindy's lead. Never said a word. Just stared, and sometimes smiled.

It was summertime, that she remembered, a very hot day. She was practising the piano in the music room. Through the French windows she could see Ted tidying the herbaceous border, bare to his slim hips. Ruth watched as she played, saw him bend and straighten, long arms brushing through the tall flowers; plucking, picking, pulling. Now and then he stepped back onto the lawn to survey his work and looked towards the house, scratching the hairs on his chest. Ruth wavered, at one moment certain he could see her, the next equally certain he could not. She stopped playing. He did not react. She began to play again, a hymn, 'Jerusalem the Golden', shouting out the words she knew he knew too: 'I know not, oh, I know not what joys await us there, what radiancy of glory, what bliss beyond compare'. He went on hoeing the weeds and whistling between his teeth, a different tune. Ruth banged the piano lid shut, and got up. Out of sight beneath the gallery she unzipped and slipped out of her school skirt; she undid the buttons of her cream blouse and took this off as well, her socks too, brown woollen knickers and Tweenage bra alone remaining. Without daring to look out Ruth took up a position by the window, in full view of Ted, and danced twice through her ballet routine. Reseated at the piano, and reclothed, Ruth turned her head in anticipated triumph towards the garden. Young Ted had disappeared.

Not long after this, a week or two, something else occurred. Unable to find Ted one afternoon in any of his usual places, Ruth wondered if he might be working on the crown, and, hurrying along the top of the ha-ha, she made straight for the stile. Half-way along she suddenly noticed him below her in the deep ditch, his head within a yard of her feet. Ted was looking up, frowning, and between his legs he held in both hands his extended penis, the size and stature, it occurred to Ruth in retrospect, of a donkey's.

'Afternoon, Miss,' he said.

For the rest of that adolescent summer, wherever she went Ruth felt young Ted's eyes upon her. He always seemed to be there, everywhere. In church. In the crowd on Sports Day at Shepton High. At her elbow in the ten-pin bowling alley at Eastney Fair. Following her. He must have been following her. And there he was at the Priory, day after day, clearly visible from every window. Leering behind the hedge. Beckoning, nodding, rubbing his crutch.

Ted never touched her, though. At least young Ted had never touched her. She had that to be thankful for. Mustn't forget that.

By the beginning of the summer it had become established daily practice for Ruth to collect Gabriel from play-school and take him home with her to the Priory for lunch; on two afternoons a week she kept him till after tea. Having Gabs to play with every day was a joy unlike anything Ruth had ever experienced. He was running around now, and talking faster than he could think. Ruth adored him; and he adored her, calling her Jo-the-Po – whatever that meant – and making her laugh whenever too long a period of time had elapsed since the last joke. Gabriel was an inventive child and contributed almost as much as Ruth to the imaginary world they created at story-time on the balcony of the gazebo, to which they often escaped for an afternoon nap in

Dad's hammock. The scarlet knight had returned from the Crusades bringing all sorts of odd travellers to entertain the throng: Daryll the Dwarf was a firm favourite; and Juniper the baby Indian elephant who fanned the princess with his ears; there was Jelly Belly Johnson too, on loan from Disneyland; and the knight's much abused lisping Saracen slave, Wabin bin Huthi. The sounds were what mattered most to Ruth and Gabriel, not the sense, and the crown of beeches rang out all summer long with their playful shouts.

Rather than spend every evening closeted with Mum at the Priory, Ruth was often to be found with Twinkle and her parents, or over at the Fitzgeralds. Mrs Fitzgerald was alone in Lee House for the three mid-week nights her husband spent in town, and Ruth took care to call on those evenings only, bicycling round by the road. All Ruth wanted was someone outside to talk to, someone prepared to answer her endless questions. That this someone could be Mrs Fitzgerald whom she knew so well and trusted so completely, was an unsought bonus. They mostly sat in the bay window of the morning room, Ruth with her back to the view, watching the sun set in Mrs Fitzgerald's green eyes.

Mrs Fitzgerald adjusted the velvet cushion on which she was resting her crippled leg, and poured herself another cup of coffee.

'It's a mixed blessing of course. There are lots of things I haven't done because of the children. Things I'd like to have done if it had all been different. Childless. I don't think I'd've minded.'

Having absorbed Ruth's barrage of questions on childbirth, changing nappies, change of life, and anything else connected with dreams of motherhood, it was Mrs Fitzgerald's turn to speak her mind.

'You seem to think having babies and being in love are the same thing. Very naïve. Dangerous too at your age. It would be good for you to fall in love. But for God's sake don't go and have a baby till you're absolutely sure. Of yourself, not of the man. Frankly I've never thought it mattered too much which man it was.'

Mrs Fitzgerald pinched her lips between thumb and forefinger, a girlhood gesture never abandoned.

'Not that I've tried many, I'm glad to say. If it doesn't matter that much, there's no point in changing, is there? Fitz and I have the children, we don't need each other as well.' She paused. 'Look at Conor, he's got the right idea.'

'Conor?' Ruth queried.

'Yes, your Conor. He married a wife and mother, not a lover. And he'll be happy. So will she for that matter.'

'That's what I said to him. In my letter. I said . . . well, that's what I said.'

Mrs Fitzgerald smiled. It was almost dark.

'You know, there's nothing wrong with you, so don't panic. You feel things more deeply than others, that's all. You're cleverer than most of them too, so you can't be fooled. You are right. You're absolutely right to be shocked by the world. What sane woman isn't? But you can learn to cope.'

'Yes?'

'Don't you feel it yourself?'

'Yes. I do right now. I just, well, it doesn't matter.'

'What, dear?'

'You know.'

'Do I?'

Ruth was fiddling with a loose tongue of leather on the arm of the chair. 'I told you before,' she mumbled.

'Tell me again,' Mrs Fitzgerald quietly requested.

'I want to be loved. By a boy.'

'Give it time. You've only just begun, remember. You've only just begun to be a woman. Because of your illness.'

'Perhaps it's too late.'

'Nonsense!'

Ruth looked unconvinced; she sat staring silently at Mrs Fitzgerald, her eyes, her whole body pleading for reassurance.

'Goodness me, there's no set order to life. We all learn different things at different times. Some women learn to make love when they're eighteen, others when they're forty. The same with the intellect. Remember what a silly boy Conor was? He's grown up a bit now, but he still doesn't understand life half as well as you do.'

'Lucky him.' A note of anger had crept into Ruth's voice, mixed with self-pity.

'Now, now, Ruthie, I won't have that. You're not the only

person in the world who worries about sex. Look at Graham.'

'*Graham?*' Ruth blinked, forcing her narrow field of vision to widen out, until Mrs Fitzgerald's second son entered the frame. She could barely see him: a slim, dark boy balancing a croquet mallet on his toe, a half-smile fixed shyly on his face. 'What's wrong with Graham?'

Mrs Fitzgerald did not reply immediately. She had been ambushed by her own much more accessible images: of a young man, the brightest of her three boys, running away to Canada. 'Nothing. Never mind.'

'He looked alright at the wedding.'

'Yes, he's fine, I expect.'

'What then?'

'Well, only that he needs help too, rather like you do, Ruthie dear. Though not in hospital, I'm glad to say.'

'From a psychiatrist?'

'Yes. Actually he's had treatment for years. Still goes every week.' Mrs Fitzgerald adjusted her leg again on its cushion, and laughed. 'It's rather sweet. When he's travelling he takes along a portable tape recorder and talks to his doctor. They send each other tapes. Must be rather nice, don't you think?'

'I wouldn't know what to say . . . Hello, Dr Cardy, it's me. I've just had tea. The damson jam was mouldy. Mum's thinking of dyeing her hair. What colour do you think it should be? Blue? . . . It doesn't work. By the time you get the reply it's always too late. Mum would already be pink!'

They both laughed. Mrs Fitzgerald wagged a friendly finger, and allowed a more serious expression to return to her face. 'It's *never* too late, dear.'

'No, I know. I won't give up, I promise.'

'Relax. Give it time.'

'Yes, I must. It's so slow though. And everything's so fragmented. I can never stick the pieces together, that's my trouble. The pieces never seem to fit together.'

Later that same week Ruth and Twinkle were sitting on a rug in the shade of the Fare's pear tree, Gabriel asleep between them. Twinkle and her parents lived at the centre of Watham in two stone-built cottages knocked into one, mother and daughter sharing a large studio in what had once been the village forge.

Their working methods were very different, the mother destroying half her delicate pots after firing, the daughter rejecting nothing. According to Twinkle the act of work itself defined the worth of the product, and everything she made was always put to use.

'Why haven't you ever told me about Gabs' father?' Ruth asked, slightly aggressively.

'You never asked.'

'I am now'.

Twinkle adjusted the layers of lace-trimmed skirt in her lap. She was sitting with her legs crossed, slim and flat chested, straight hair gathered in an old-fashioned black net. 'His name's Richard. Richard Girschon. You may've heard of him?' Ruth shook her head. 'No? He's quite well-known now. He was a friend of a friend at the Ruskin, and I've never told him about Gabriel. That's all there is to tell.'

'Don't tease, please. I'm serious.'

'So am I. Look, he's an American poet. I met him at a Commem. ball. I liked him and we had sex. In the summer vac I saw him again, but he was completely different. Stuck up. Interested only in himself. I haven't seen him since and never want to. Will that do?'

Ruth licked her lips.

'Poor Gabs,' she eventually said. 'No Dad.'

Twinkle brushed a flying beetle from her arm.

'Won't do him any harm. Children belong to their mothers.'

That night, lying in her bed close to the open window, Ruth thought about the things Twinkle had told her. Twinkle had made love to a strange man at an Oxford ball. Where else? How many times?

Once was enough to make a baby.

Poor Gabs. Poor, poor Gabs. Don't worry, my little love. I'm here, don't worry. I'll look after you. You can rely on me. I love you, I do. Let me be your Dad, please do.

I am a bit already.

All summer Ruth was unstoppable. She seemed to be everywhere at once: leading a sing-song in the minibus on the way home from the disableds' June outing; taking over Bible classes when Reverend Hibbs' sister went into hospital to have her veins done; helping Mrs Cornish create a bigger bring-and-buy cake display than the oldest old hands at the WI had ever seen before. Nothing seemed too much trouble for her.

'Are you sure you're alright? You've lost so much weight. Never see you these days,' Mum complained to Ruth one evening, after a particularly hectic week in September.

'Come on, Mum, do I look ill? Honestly now. Do I?'

'You don't look well, that's all I can say,' her mother replied, tossing her head and looking away. 'You'll wear yourself out and be ill again. I know you. Good Lord, if anyone knows you I do! You're different. You can't live like that. You'll be ill.'

'Not this time. Not this time I won't,' Ruth replied.

Mum's back was turned, to hide the tears. Ruth kissed the furrowed side of her mother's neck, and went upstairs. It was early, barely nine o'clock. Face half-washed, teeth again unbrushed, Ruth knelt on the rag rug at the side of her bed and began her prayers, first, as always, remembering Dad: 'For those who have passed into the marvellous light of Thy presence, we give Thee thanks, O Lord.'

Then the twenty-third Psalm followed by the Lord's Prayer, both recited out loud in a clear voice.

'Thine is the day, O Lord,' Ruth concluded her formal prayers. 'And Thine is the night. Grant that the sun of Righteousness may abide in our hearts to drive away the darkness of evil thoughts. Amen.'

Ruth let her hands drop from in front of her face and laid them at rest on the patchwork bedspread. Opening her eyes she stared out of the window and, still on her knees, continued her private conversation.

I don't want to upset Mum, Goddi. Couldn't you explain to her? She'll believe you, if you tell her nicely. If you explain to her how it's for the best.

I'm not deserting her. I'm not, am I?

I've got to have a life of my own. Surely she understands that. A family of my own.

I know it used to be all I wanted, to paint and to be with Mum. It's difficult for Mum, I can see that. For years she's done nothing but look after me. Hand and foot. She's done it, she's won! Doesn't she understand?

Can't she see I'm getting better?
I am, aren't I, Goddi?
Aren't I?

'It's all in pieces, Twinkle.'
'Is it?'
'Yes. Quite big pieces . . . And smaller pieces too. More and more pieces. All flying around.'
'Like outer space?'
'Inside my head.'
'Can't you make them into a pattern, or something?'
'No, I can't, I *can't*,' Ruth screeched.

Ruth and Twinkle were in the studio, still wearing their coats after a walk; it was the first day of November and the weather had broken, ending Ruth's long Indian summer.

'Couldn't you start painting again?' Twinkle asked.

Head bowed, Ruth tried to think what it might be like to return to her work.

How? For what?

The only thing she wanted to paint, she couldn't. She'd tried on canvas hundreds of times, thousands of times in her mind.

Such a simple scene. Why was it so difficult to paint?

A dark green wide-bellied rowing boat close to the spring shore of Dad's lake; the sky clear, the water ruffled by a slight breeze; a man resting on the oars, smiling at the small figure of a girl in the stern; Dad's face, her back; the crown of beeches in the distance; a swallow looping freedom in the air.

'There's nothing to paint,' she said. 'It's all in pieces. Fragments of metal. Of glass. Whirling around. None of it fits together.'

'You could go to Paul Furness. Work with him again?'
'He wouldn't have me.'
'He might. No harm in asking.'
'I wouldn't last a day,' Ruth insisted, and raised her head to stare straight into Twinkle's eyes, challenging her friend to tell the truth.

'No, perhaps you wouldn't,' Twinkle admitted, and kissed Ruth on the cheek. 'What'll you do?'

'Go back to Dr Cardy, I expect. This month, next month, sometime, never,' she chanted.

'Do you mind?'

'Not really. Once it gets really bad there's nowhere else I can go.'

'You wouldn't try and see it through at home?'

'No, I'll never get better at home.'

'Why not?'

'Because . . . because . . .' She seemed on the verge of finding the answer, but it suddenly escaped. 'I don't know,' she concluded, in a voice of utter hopelessness.

Twinkle frowned. She was standing by the verandah windows, looking onto the view that was so intimately Ruth's, crowned by the ten old beeches.

'Do you remember team selection at school, Jo?' she asked.

'Yes?'

'You were usually one of the team captains.'

'Everyone else was so *hopeless*,' Ruth asserted.

'I certainly was. I was always the very last to be chosen.'

'Were you, Twink?'

'Don't you remember? Even if it meant having an extra player no one wanted me on their side. You too, Jo. You never used to choose me either. You must remember.'

'You didn't like games.'

'That's not true. I just wasn't any good at them.'

'Then why did you pretend to be ill?'

'Because I couldn't *bear* never to be chosen, not even by you.'

Ruth had joined Twinkle by the window. She put her arm round her friend's shoulders, shocked out of her own immediate anguish by Twinkle's sad little story. 'Why didn't you tell me?' she asked.

'I did. But you never listened.'

The essence of Twinkle's childhood suffering burst into Ruth's heightened consciousness, and she closed her eyes, bowed her head. 'How did you stand feeling so miserable?' she moaned.

'I just did.'

In time Ruth stopped her moaning and stared long at the crown of beeches. 'You just do,' she eventually said. 'And I just don't. That's the difference, isn't it? But I can't, I really can't.'

'I know . . . It's not fair.'

There were tears in Twinkle's eyes as she spoke.

PART
II

Excerpts from the 'Ruth' tape recordings made by
Graham Fitzgerald

Thirteenth of February. You asked me to tell you more
about my visit to Ruth Harrison. And you're right, I
suppose; it has set some hidden thoughts on the move.
I couldn't understand why Mother wanted *me* to go,
rather than Conor or Mirabel.
Because I had the time to spare, she said; and was already
in London. She flattered me, too. Told me I was the best
person for the job.
'But Mother, I hardly know Ruth Harrison,' I tried to tell
her.
'Don't be ridiculous. Of course you do, you've known her
since she was a child. And take her a basket of peaches
please.'
'Peaches? At this time of year?'
'Then grapes, I don't mind. Or clementines. Goodness,
you make such a *meal* of everything.'
See? She hasn't changed. No argument. No dialogue.
Still just as impatient with me.
It's true, though; I have known Ruth since she was a
child. She must've been about four when the Harrisons
bought the Priory. I would have been twelve, John
fourteen, Mirabel six, and Conor five. It's difficult for me
to place childhood memories precisely in context. I'm not
sure I took much notice of her at the time. In my mind,

though, I've a picture of the liveliest creature imaginable. She was noisy and naughty, and everyone adored her. She used to be so pretty too, I remember. Still is, I think, in a different way.

Wait a minute, I've written some of this down. So I wouldn't forget to tell you anything important. I'll just get my notes.

That's better.

When you've lived abroad for as long as I have, it's strange, but London ceases to look English any more. To you foreigners the red double-deckers and the dome of St Paul's and Big Ben, things like that have, I suppose, a particular Englishness. Not to me. To me they are all negative signs. They tell me I am not at home in Vancouver; that I'm not in Chicago, or Marseilles, or Cairo (not that I've ever been to Cairo). Positive Englishness resides in more secret places: in a room with stained floorboards framing a worn Persian carpet, a Broadwood baby grand in the bay window, and loose-covered comfy chairs scattered about the hearth; brass coal tongs and a matching hairless brush are far more English than . . . than Buckingham Palace, if you like. You see, on my way to visit Ruth I came across a scene which struck me as being *so* English. Armed with Father's disintegrating A to Z, I had turned right out of Bethnal Green Station down Three Colts Lane, and left into Cambridge Heath Road. From there it looked like a simple fifteen-minute walk to All Souls, via either Roman Road or Old Ford Road. (I used to think proper names had inalienable physical properties until I met a surveyor who came from an Eastney in British Columbia and was also called Fitzgerald! Cavell Ward, All Souls Hospital, Trafalgar Gardens could just as easily've been in Calcutta, I suppose, or Boston.) Keeping a weather eye on the map, I almost missed the marvellous scene in the park opposite – behind cast-iron railings on the tarmac of a multi-purpose municipal playground, a dozen women were having a game of netball.

Put like that it probably sounds nothing special, but it was, I assure you. I wish I had the skill to express how special it was. Its very ordinariness made it special, if you see what I mean. The fact that it was happening here, in a corner of the East End, without anyone paying any attention at all. So natural. So wholesome. The breathless calls of the young women. 'Drat!' 'Pass, for Pete's sake.' 'Topping.' They were mostly quite big girls. In navy-blue pleated sports skirts joined between the legs. (Mirabel had some for lacrosse at Wickham, but I've forgotten what they're called. Not jodhpurs.) Several of them had badges stitched to the breast pockets of their shirts. Aertex shirts, you know? The teams were distinguished by coloured sashes, the purple and yellow tails dancing at their hips as they galloped from end to end. There was no referee, that I recall. And no arguments. Where else but in England would you see women playing netball in a public park during lunch hour? In New York it wouldn't be safe. Dirty old men would stick their dicks through the wire.

All Souls looks more like a House at school than a hospital, a gothicky building with its dripping lime in the forecourt and a double-sided flight of steps leading up to the porch. After watching the netball I was feeling more confident about my visit.

A patient in a yellow dressing-gown stood with her nose and hands pressed flat against the glass panel of the inside door. 'Push' it said, so I pushed. She shuffled aside to let me in. A black porter was sitting at a desk at the end of the hall. He had a dog-eared notebook in front of him. There was a pencil, I remember, attached by a piece of string to the spiral spine. I asked for Cavell Ward and was directed up a flight of three steps to his left. Thank you, I said, giving him my name.

I asked if I should sign the book.

He stared at me; one of his eyes was bloodshot. He got up from behind his desk, shaking his head, and guided me by the elbow down the passage and up the three stone steps. We were standing outside a pair of sickly green doors with bulls-eye panels of glass giving a distorted view through to the brightly sunlit interior. He pointed to the door and nodded, patting me on the back of the head as though I was an imbecile. I thanked him again, glad to get away.

The ward was bathed in sunlight from tall windows running down both sides of the room. There were ten or fifteen beds, and about the same number of people. The shapeless forms seemed part of the furniture. I looked from face to face: young women, old women, some up and dressed, others lying in bed, all staring at me without a sign of recognition. Which was Ruth? Could she have changed so much? The nurse sitting at a formica table in the centre of the room came to my rescue. (There was a nearly completed giant jigsaw on the table, of Turner's 'Fighting Temeraire'.)

'Can I help?'

Her voice was friendly and relaxed. I realised the threatening silence could only have lasted a second or two, the stillness perhaps less, as I soon caught the constant mutter of troubled voices and saw the ceaseless shaking of worried heads.

'Thanks. I'm looking for Ruth Harrison,' I said.

'Ru-uth. A vis-it-or,' the nurse called out. 'That's her bed. There in the corner behind the screens. Silly girl always does this at visiting time.'

You know, I still feel now exactly as I did then: that my turning up uninvited at Ruth's bedside was a terrible intrusion. If it hadn't worked out it would've been *entirely* Mother's fault. You can't do that to people. One has no right to interfere like that, willy-nilly. Mother thinks everyone always wants to be helped. They don't. Some people want to help themselves. I, for one, think it's better to fail on your own than let anyone try to help you through. It never works anyway. And you can take it on your own. The failures. The disappointments. It doesn't hurt so much on one's own.

I don't count you. Your help's different. Not like asking a friend.

Some people say a problem shared is a problem halved, don't they?

Not me. I think it's a problem doubled.

I've lost my place. Wait.

Here we are.

'Ruth?' I called, standing behind the flimsy screen. (I had to bow my head so as not to see over the top.)

There was no answer and I called louder.

'Yes? Who is it?' came the throaty reply.

'Graham, Graham Fitzgerald. I've brought you a present from Mother.'

I heard the rustle of papers and the clunk of a plastic beaker replaced on the bedside cupboard; then Ruth's step across the parquet floor. A hand grasped the screen nearest me. There was a pause before a sudden movement sent it concertinaing to the side on rubber wheels. Ruth stood in front of me, four feet away, arms open wide, a broad child's smile on her bloated face. I may have hesitated. I must have I, suppose, for the look of appeal deepened behind those dark eyes of hers, magnified by the spectacles on that idiotic lurex cord. I opened my arms to her – what else could I have done? She pulled her spectacles from her nose, lowered her head as though to charge, and stepped in to press her forehead against my chest; with my hands I patted her back; and with her hands she clung to my shoulders.

I stayed about twenty minutes, sitting on the chair beside her bed. She clasped my hand in hers all the while, lying fully clothed on the bed, eyes shut. She tried to talk, but obviously found it a strain, and I told her there was no need. I said very little myself. There was very little one could say.

'You must go now. Go! I can't take you any more,' she said in the end. And I left, promising to come back later in the week.

Tenth of March. It's difficult for me to recall exactly what I thought of Ruth's state of mind on that first afternoon in Bethnal Green: I know so much more than I did a few weeks ago.

What did it feel like without knowing what I do now?

An impossible question.

Mind you, I've never been one of those who look upon Ruth Harrison's breakdowns as temporary; as temporary

aberrations in an otherwise normal life. I've always feared
that for Ruth herself it's precisely the other way round.
That for her, the agony is continuous, the peace illusory.
Seeing her in All Souls confirmed my worst suspicions:
this is really how she feels all the time, inside the outside.
I don't blame the others – Mother and the rest of the
village, least of all her own mother – for failing to see the
truth. It's easy enough for me to be realistic because I'm
never there; she's never my responsibility. I don't have to
greet her with a smile in church on Sundays, pass the
time of day in the Post Office on Mondays. I've never
once been into her studio. I don't think I've even sat
down at the same table for a meal with Ruth since before
her first breakdown, when she was seventeen, three
months before I left for Canada.

One of the reasons Ruth and I get on so well, the main
reason probably, is my refusal to pretend everything's
alright. I must be the only person from home she can talk
to openly without being frightened of her own pain
wounding them.

My God, is she honest with me. Brutally honest.

I haven't told you what happened on my second visit,
have I?

'I don't think I thanked you properly for the tangerines,'
she said. 'Were they tangerines?'

'Clementines actually. They're from Mother anyway, not
me,' I said.

We were sitting on a bench in the miniature shrubbery of
nearby Victoria Park. It's a sheltered spot and the
lukewarm sun kept us cosy enough, well wrapped up in
gloves and scarves.

'Probably not. Probably mandarins,' she said.

'Mandarins are Chinese bank managers,' I said, laughing
at my own joke.

I expected a characteristic cackle from Ruth, but she had
stopped listening and was gripping the scarred park
bench with both hands, staring at the earth between her
knees. I instantly regretted leaving the safety of the
hospital grounds.

'You don't still blame your mother, do you Gray? You

mustn't. It wasn't her fault. She's the Lord's servant,
working His mysteries.' Ruth looked at me, searching my
face.
'Was that why you ran away?' she continued.
'What do you mean? I didn't run away, anyway.'
'You did, Gray, you did. You're still running.'
(That's another thing about her. She seems to know
things about me I hardly know myself. She's always
doing it, just when I'm beginning to fear she really might
be mad.)
'It's your own fault. You expected too much of your
mother. She's quite a woman but she's not perfect. No
one's perfect, you know.' She laid a gloved hand on mine.
'Mum forgave her years ago. Why can't you?'
I must've jerked my head around and stared, for she gave
me a derisive snort before going on.
'Dear me, no need to look so shocked. We're not *children*.
Dad told me all about it. He always did. All about all of
them. Before I really knew what it meant actually. It
eased his conscience. Like the Catholics and confession.'
The shit! What he did was bad enough, but to confide in
his daughter too? The bastard. No wonder she's screwed
up. Always so charming and helpful; the gracious and
good Mat Harrison. Balls! I saw through you, you . . .
you filthy piece of shit.

Twentieth of March. Why are you so interested in the
Ruth business?
I suppose you know what you're about.
You're right, too. It still makes me incredibly angry.
That's one thing I'll never get over; hearing about those
conscience-saving chats with his daughter.
I forgave Mother ages ago. It didn't last long anyway; and
she was very discreet. Maybe I did run away from her,
but if I did it certainly wasn't from her failure in my eyes,
but from mine in hers.
No, it's Harrison I can't forgive. His self-righteousness.
And the way he tried to act the country gentleman. He
wasn't, not by a long chalk. Came from nowhere.
Not that it matters. He earnt every penny of what was

his, I don't begrudge him that.

But why couldn't he be that and be thankful? Why did he want to run half Somerset as well? They made such a fool of him, extracting money in return for meaningless titles. Honorary Vice-President of the Radstock Beagles. I ask you! Probably only poked their wives for form's sake too. Silly bastard.

Twenty-first of March. I've never known exactly what's wrong with Ruth. Actually, I quite often wonder if there really is anything wrong at all. Sure, something must've caused the original breakdown – she became desperately thin, I remember. Like a skeleton. And worked idiotically hard for A levels she could've passed standing on her head.

Collapsed from weakness the first day of exams.

But what do they mean by 'chemical imbalance'? They've pumped her so full of drugs over the years that *of course* her body needs them now. Her mind doesn't, though. For someone who lives such an isolated life, experiencing so little of the world, she understands a helluva lot. I don't think I've ever met anyone with Ruth's innate wisdom. Anyone with a clearer awareness of the essence of human nature. She's a sort of sage.

Perhaps I should ask the doctors at All Souls the truth while I've got the chance?

No. It would feel like going behind her back, as though I don't trust her.

Whose truth anyway? Hers or theirs?

Ruth isn't a liar. What she says she feels is what she *does* feel, however impossible this sometimes sounds to me.

Second of April. I stayed up in town last weekend, and Ruth asked me to meet her and her mother for tea in the Strand. They were late, and instead of coming straight inside they stood on the pavement and made faces at me through the window, like a couple of schoolgirls. Mrs Harrison had a funny hat on, her watery eyes shielded by its old-fashioned veil. When she sat down I noticed that her short neck was angled forward like a bird's, a knot of

muscle at the back; a sign of accumulated tension, I feel.
She was heavily made-up and drops of sweat ringed her
hairline. Still, the two women are immensely happy
together, each deferring to the other at the merest hint of
disagreement; on the question of toast or scones – scones,
Mrs Harrison decided – and on the correct height of
Nelson's Column, which they could see through the café
window.

They'd spent the afternoon in the National Gallery. Ruth
couldn't believe I didn't know Paolo della Francesca's
'Nativity', proof positive, she claims, of God's presence
on earth.

I told her I like the Turners best, and she informed me
there were none there, that they are all in the Tate. (Is
that true, I wonder?)

Fifteenth of April. The other day Ruth threw a terrible
tantrum and refused to accept her discharge papers. One
of the ward sisters, a Pakistani, took her side against the
psychiatrists. Dr Cardy remained firm, though. There's
nothing more they can do, Ruth told me he'd said, now
that the scales are correctly balanced. Yesterday, on the
actual morning of her discharge, she somehow got
through to me at the laboratory, screaming and sobbing
down the phone, begging me to come immediately and
tell them how impossible it was for her to go home, how
bad it would be for her.

I didn't know what to say. I've never heard her talk like
that about the Priory. A male voice interrupted, a calm
middle-European voice – Dr Cardy's, I presume – and
apologised for any disturbance.

I went to Bethnal Green yesterday afternoon as usual
after work, imagining Ruth would still be there; rather
counting on it in fact. No, the doorman said, Miss
Harrison was no longer with them. No, Dr Cardy was not
available. A Pakistani nurse? No, all the nurses were
English.

I tried, but there was nothing I could do.

I'll miss my visits. She appreciated my coming so much. I
can see her at home of course, on the weekends I'm not

sailing. But it'll never be the same, we'll never be as close again. Times like that can never be repeated. Life never repeats itself, you always say.

Is that really so?

Telling you all this seems to help; though I'm not sure why.

It's such an effort – like an exercise at school, not like our normal tapes at all.

Did I just call Eastney home? I think I did.

I've been away too long. Two semesters is far too long; I won't do it again. I'm a scientist, not a teacher.

Twentieth of May. It's surprising how easily Ruth has readjusted to the old life, taking up her Parish duties as if nothing had happened.

Maybe nothing has happened, in her terms.

On Saturdays I quite often go over to the Priory to lend a man's hand with their labours in the garden. At All Souls Ruth never mentioned her interest in the garden; talked instead, with some enthusiasm, of getting a job; nothing too demanding at first, helping out at a Shepton tea shop or working at one of those roadside fruit stalls for a couple of hours a day. I suggested a second-hand bookshop might be more suitable and she had loved the idea. There was nothing she'd like better, she said. The answer to everything.

I hadn't seen her big painting then. I'm glad I hadn't, it's so overwhelming.

It was in the drawing room when I saw it last weekend, propped against the settee. No one uses the room any more – a grotesque monument to Mat Harrison's social mountaineering, flagged with expensive Sheraton furniture and Christmas card oils. What a horrid clever man he was . . . is; he stares out of Ruth's masterpiece, crowned in gold, bearded in silver, nose and lips as straight and narrow as the Devil's. Below him hangs the head of a bull, with human ears. On the bull's horns a fantail pigeon perches next to a nervous starling, and two voles poke their snouts out through the nostrils – sniffing the air of Ruth's limbo-land. All the faces except her father's have sunken eyes and death-drugged skins, their hands disproportionately larger and more alive than their heads.

I've no idea what it means and yet it's all compellingly familiar. Like a distant dream. As though Ruth has delved into the recesses of my thoughts and pulled out images I cannot myself see in waking hours.

That can't be so, of course. All the same the images aren't hers alone. Perhaps they belong to that land? To the Vale of Glastonbury itself? Ghosts of chivalry.

She grimaced when I told her how wonderful her painting is, dismissed the compliment with a shrug of her broad shoulders.

Eighth of November. Chicago. My last lecture tomorrow. Then home. It's been quite a successful conference really. Better than most.

Do you really need me to do the Ruth thing again? I can never see that it's getting us anywhere.

OK. I'll have a go.

Where are my notes?

Right.

If it hadn't been for Ruth I don't know how I'd've survived those five months in England. Not just in the negative sense of her keeping my mind occupied, but in the positive sense of stimulation and enjoyment.

She's marvellous company, you know, most of the time. As anxious to please as a puppy.

In fact, she's young and innocent in every way. Maybe I gave the wrong impression by describing her as a 'sage'. But she isn't quite a sprite either: too heavy in physique, too old and ill to be a sprite.

A pixie?

If I close my eyes and let my mind wander in search of an accurate image of Ruth . . . actually . . . yes, it's strange but I see the person I do know as the girl I didn't know. Didn't know really, if you see what I mean.

On the croquet pitch over at the Priory. At tournament time. We're all there, except John, who must have been married by then; and Father, who I don't think ever came. Colin Pemberton and his younger brother are in the competition, and the Boynton boy, and Cordelia and June D'Auberlay.

I must've been the oldest.

Harrison wore white flannel knicker-bockers to referee the Prince's Tournament, as he insisted on calling it. I remember – it's ridiculous, isn't it? – he used to make us go through the hoop a second time if we forgot to move our marker pegs!

There was a blackboard by the gazebo, with the names and scores in coloured chalks. And other games to play while waiting for your turn: Hoop-La on one tree, a darts board on another, and bagatelle and dominoes on the verandah. The younger kids climbed across the swooping branches of the beeches.

So did I when I was younger.

Ruth is everywhere I look, rushing about in a red dress, black pigtails banging on her shoulders.

She had this wonderful ability to make people feel their only obligation was to enjoy themselves. No, that's clumsily put. And she was probably only fourteen as I see her, fifteen at the most, and yet I'm sure she was an inspiration to us all. Her energy and enthusiasm were irresistible; you couldn't help but feel better in her presence. Life-enhancing is what she was.

I always thought Conor would marry Ruth.

Where's Mrs Harrison in my picture? I don't see her immediately. ('Inconsequentially attractive' Father once called her, à propos of nothing at all as far as I can remember.)

So different now. If I picture the Priory now, up she looms as large as life. Larger. Perpetually attendant on Ruth's beck and call.

Mrs Harrison lives, eats, breathes and sleeps Ruth. Nothing interests her in the smallest way except it be connected with Ruth.

Third of June. It's odd being in Somerset again. A year on and nothing changes. It's strange, isn't it? Nothing *seems* to change and yet nothing is ever quite the same.

Mother and Father are, to me, just what they've always been. Except on Saturday we'll be celebrating their fiftieth wedding anniversary.

That's what I hate most about Mother, I think: the way she always makes me feel like a child.

I expect everyone tells you that. I've probably told you myself. A dozen times, probably. Don't you ever get bored?

I went to see Ruth. Like you told me to.

I'm not going to use notes this time, if you don't mind. You'll get it as it comes.

Actually, I didn't see Ruth. She'd shut herself up in her bedroom. Up there at the back of the house. Mrs Harrison and I had tea on our own in the big kitchen.

It never struck me before how similar Ruth and her mother are. Not in looks – Ruth has her father's looks – in character. One moment they're talking sense and the next complete nonsense. They've got identical laughs too. With your eyes shut you wouldn't know which is which.

After tea Mrs Harrison took me into the studio to see the fresco Ruth's doing above the fireplace – a crucifixion.

'It is a wee bit macabre.'

I can't quite do her voice. Christ, it is macabre, though! 'It *is* a wee bit macabre.' That's better. 'Not my idea of the Son of God. Ruthie says it's a twentieth-century icon.'

Then she reeled off a whole load of names. Pierre Trudeau, John Lennon, Armstrong, the astronaut, President Kennedy, Sean Connery. And that other actor fellow, Paul Scofield. Apparently Ruth's mad about him too. Placido Domingo, Bob Dylan, Daniel Martin. And masses more. 'Sir Somebody Sober,' old Mrs Harrison says. 'As in "sober as a judge". A cricketer. I ask you! David Hockney, there's another one. Now how can he be a Christ figure?' Never waits for a reply; bangs on regardless. 'Twinkle says he's a homosexual. Is he, Graham?'

Out she comes with it, just like that. 'I wouldn't know,' I said. 'Wouldn't you?' she said. 'Ah well, doesn't matter. She's only used his hair.'

She's quite a hoot. I had to laugh. *She* was laughing like anything. You see, Ruth had given her Jesus the biggest penis you've ever seen in your life!

'Proves her heart's in the right place,' Mrs Harrison says. Great, isn't she?

Then she goes and follows it with a piece of madness. 'And how about you? How's your love-life these days? You should settle for Ruth. She's very fond of you.' Near enough word for word. You'd imagine she must've been joking, but she wasn't; she was deadly serious.

Then, as quick as lightning, she said something which literally took my breath away. She was pointing at the fresco. 'That's real blood. Ruthie killed one of the hens and spattered its blood across the wall. Who'll put up with that when I'm gone? Only a husband. Marriage is her only chance.'

How can she be so brave? How can she accept it? Her daughter doing that? And still she sees a future for her. There isn't; not a normal future. It's too late. There's too much violence stored up inside.

It's amazing what some people can endure, isn't it? They reach the very limit of endurance, and then somehow go way beyond.

I don't think there's anything in the world Ruth could do that her mother wouldn't accept.

Seventh of June. I still haven't seen Ruth. I've rung several times, but she won't even come to the phone.

'Sorry, I'm afraid she's sick today,' Mrs Harrison says. There's always a lot of muttering at their end. And once I heard Ruth scream.

My mother knows something I'm sure. Why doesn't she tell me?

I refuse to ask.

Anyway, I don't need to now. This afternoon I went round to see Mrs Cornish, the Harrisons' cleaning lady. She's tremendous. All dimples and smiles, and as fat as anything. She saw me before I even got to the gate and came waddling down the path to meet me. 'Ooh, Mr Graham, I'm mighty glad to see you. What a pallava up at

the Priory. What can us do? Lordy be!' I'm not trying to
be comic; it's how she speaks; a Somerset brogue you can
cut with a knife. She kept darting glances from side to
side, as if we were on enemy territory instead of standing
at her own front gate.
I asked her what had happened.
'Only last week it were. No, week before. That's right,
Tuesday, 'cos I were doin' the brass. Such a noise!
Proper pandominion. Screechin' and hollerin' and
bangin'. All manner of carryin' on.
'Was when I heard the glass go, I said to myself, Mrs C, I
said, you best be gettin' up them stairs sharpish and see
what's what!
'You never seed such a sight in your life, Mr Graham.
Every stick of furniture smashed to smithereens.
Curtains, patchwork bedspread, they was all torn
asunder, so help me God. And that wardrobe of hers,
why she'd throwd that on its head as tho' 'twere made of
matchsticks! There she were hollerin' at the top of her
voice: Out! Out! Out! As she throwd them bits and
pieces out of the window.
'Weren't open, mind, the window! Lord no, weren't
open!'
Frightening, isn't it? Ruth *is* frightening when she gets in
a state. And she's terribly strong now, not like she was as
a child. She's got the shoulders of a cross-channel
swimmer.
Mrs Cornish hadn't finished her story.
'Anyroads she stop when she see me. Frothin' at the
mouth. Looked like the Devil hisself our little Ruthie did,
swear to God.
'I talked to her, all calm like tho' my heart were thumpin'
no mistake. And Mrs H she phones Dr Fletcher.
Anyroads, he come quick enough and got the ole syringe
at her and we puts her to bed in the front room.'
Poor old dear, she shed a tear. Patted her cheeks with a
corner of her apron.
She said she'd remember that day as long as she lived.
There've been other things.
The night of our party Mrs Cornish was woken at two in

the morning by a terrible banging sound up at the Priory.
A booming kind of bang. Regular, she said. She got
Cornish out of bed and sent him up to see what was going
on. But apparently the noise had stopped by the time he
got there. The lights were on in the hall, though, and he
rang the bell. Mrs Harrison came to the door in her
nightie; told him to go back to bed and not to make such a
fuss.
It doesn't surprise me. Not really.
Well, to be honest, I'm a bit shocked by the chicken-
killing business. The rest doesn't surprise me at all, though
Don't forget I saw Ruth day after day at All Souls. I've
seen her crawling across the floor howling. Clinging to a
nurse's ankles begging for a dose of drugs.
I've seen three attendants, all men, struggle to hold her
down.
And what about the things she told me? You know she
used to lock herself into the craft room and masturbate
with a pipe of Dr Cardy's she'd stolen? So she told me.
And she once described – in detail – drowning a litter of
kittens in the lake at home. Pushing them one by one
through a hole in the ice.
I never mentioned that, did I?
Just because I don't talk about these things doesn't mean
they don't happen. Or that I ignore them. I don't. It's
just nicer to look on the bright side. The black side's there
though. All the time. The 'dark night of the soul', Ruth
calls it.
I'll never forget what she wrote to me once: 'Life is
almost total darkness with but one light by which one is
made into the thing one makes.'
Is that the Bible? With Ruth you never know whether it's
her or God.
Should I just call round at the Priory unannounced?
I wish I could telephone you. Why aren't I allowed to
telephone you while I'm away?
Damn it, I'm going round tomorrow.

Eighth of June. It was awful. I don't know how to tell
you.

I just walked in through the yard door. At tea time.
They were both in the kitchen, sitting at the table. Ruth
looked dreadful. That grey look. You know. Unwashed.
Hair lifeless. I could see she was seriously ill. Anybody
could have.
I kissed her all the same. On the cheek.
Apologised for not seeing her before.
Explained that I'd called round on my first day and
telephoned a lot since.
She replied quite calmly, considering. Said she knew,
that it didn't matter. Said she hadn't been well.
I can't remember what we talked about. The party, I
suppose. Ruth hardly spoke a word, and Mrs Harrison
and I had to keep on talking. Gibberish, probably.
When Ruth got up to refill the teapot we stopped. I was
listening to her in the scullery. Running some water.
Filling the electric kettle. I even heard the flick of the
switch.
Then silence. Nothing. I looked behind me, but couldn't
see round the corner into the scullery.
Such utter silence.
Then, a barely audible groan; the clatter of a knife on the
stone floor; and the shriek of a chair pushed across the
flags.
Mrs Harrison and I both jumped to our feet, and ran.
I couldn't think what had happened at first. Ruth was
lying on the floor, smiling. I smiled back.
Then I noticed she was clutching her stomach, and saw
the blood spreading across the floor.
I'm afraid to tell you what happened next.
I was sick, physically sick. In the corner, by the big bin.

Fourteenth of June. God protects His own; I no longer
doubt that. Four inches of carving knife steel passed into
Ruth's stomach and damaged nothing, not her kidneys
nor spleen nor intestine, nothing. She lost a lot of blood,
of course. And sported a nice collection of stitches; but
they discharged her from Bath General in three days.
Sent her over to the pyschiatric hospital at Dilham Park
on Tuesday.

Now *that's* a tough place, I can tell you. Nothing like All Souls.

Vast and isolated and impersonal. An expanded Edwardian pile, still with its original wrought-iron gates. Guards stop you at a crash barrier, take your name and the number-plate of your car. I couldn't find my way actually. Masses of blue signposts point in confusing directions. Past rows of rusty oxygen cylinders. And ambulances with flat tyres. So disorganised.

I eventually found the main entrance and a receptionist told me Ruth was in Ward Q5. At the north end of the East Wing. There was a wire-glass door to the East Wing, with two orderlies stopping people from going in. Stopping patients getting out, really, I suppose. One of them told me Ruth was waiting in the Visitors' Room.

I knocked, and pushed open the swing door.

What would you have expected?

She was sitting on a black plastic settee, low down. She tried to get up but a stab of pain sent her reeling. Her eyes were closed. The lips moved in her pale face, silently, as though she was praying. In an odd way, she looked quite well; not twisted and crooked as she sometimes does. When her eyes opened they were calm. Calmer than I can ever remember seeing them. And not from drugs, I don't think.

I asked her how she was feeling.

'At peace, Gray,' she said. 'At peace. I've got rid of it all now. Everything's going to be fine now.'

That day we talked for an hour. And all afternoon yesterday and today. She talks such sense, you know. It really does seem this anguished act of self-mutilation might have done the trick. When you get so close to death and survive, I imagine it proves life is worth living. With her religious kick, she puts it differently. She said something about having been foolish enough to put God to the test. And that He, in His infinite mercy, had shown her how much He loves her. With the certainty of God's love she claims that any amount of suffering is bearable. For salvation, she says, you can wait till the end of the world.

I believe her. Who wouldn't?
Even you'd have believed her. She made *such* sense.
I've got to believe her.
For my sake as well as hers, I've got to believe she's going
to get better.

Twentieth of December. I'll be in Pittsburgh a couple
more days, testing the bits of fuselage they recovered
yesterday.
Bad news about Ruth, I'm afraid. The office sent on a
letter from Mother.
And don't say I told you so, or wishful thinking or
whatever. I *said* they should never have sent her back to
the Priory. From Dilham she should've gone to a
halfway-house, or whatever they call them. They
could've got her a job, helped her learn to look after
herself, see a bit of life. She's marvellous with people,
they know that. She could've done some community
work. Still could.
What do they expect? Stuck away in that dreary house
with her mother. Mourning the memory of that awful
man.
I suppose you'd say it's necessary; that if anger's there it's
better that it comes out.
I don't blame Ruth. Fussed over like a child. How else
could she get away? Jesus, she must've been at her wit's
end.
No . . . No, that's wrong . . . I feel sorry for Mrs
Harrison, I really do. At least she's going to be alright.
Concussion and some nasty bruising.
It could've been far worse. She might easily have been
killed.
Ruth's back in Dilham.
Perhaps it'll be for the best in the end. I mean, Ruth
certainly won't be able to go home again now. And having
no alternative she might actually find it easier to make a
life for herself. I'm sure she can. In spite of everything
that's happened.
A restricted life, but her own.
Give it time. That's what you'd say, isn't it?

How long, though? How *long*?
'Well, we'll see. Rome wasn't built in a day.'
That's what you'll say.
I can hear you saying it.

PART
III

1

'Mum? Mum, it's me.' Ruth shouted down the telephone.

No reply except the sound, instantly recognisable to Ruth, of her mother breathing in sharply through her upturned nose, and more slowly out.

'It's you. I thought they said it was Sylvia. Never mind. How are you?'

'I'm fine. How are you?'

'Much better thank you. Yes, I'm fine now.'

Mrs Harrison was in her ice-blue cubicle at Bath General Hospital. It was three days since the 'accident', as she already referred to it, the first on which she had been allowed up – for a frame-assisted totter to the bathroom. She was sitting in a cane tub-chair wedged between the end of her bed and the wall; a nurse had wheeled in the telephone trolley and plugged it in at her side.

It was the first time they had spoken since Ruth had attacked her mother in bed in the early hours of the morning and beaten her unconscious with the back of a dustpan-brush, immediately after which Ruth had summoned two ambulances, one for her mother and one for herself – to deliver herself back into the hands of the psychiatrists at Dilham.

'I'm glad of the rest,' Mum said.

'I sprained my wrist,' Ruth replied, and they both laughed. 'Don't tell anyone, will you?'

'Tell anyone what?'

'That it's me. They told me I wasn't to ring you.'

Again a sharp intake of breath.

'How did you get my number?'

'I knew it. From when I was there. Easy – Bath nine eight double eight. I told them I was ringing Twinkle. She came to see me yesterday. And Gabs.'

'That's nice.'

'Yes, it was. Lovely.'

A longer pause.

'You mustn't feel bad about what happened. Please, Ruthie. I know you couldn't help it. It's the pills. They must've given you the wrong pills. It wasn't you. You know that, don't you?'

'Oh Mum, Mum!' Ruth shrieked down the telephone. 'I love you so much. I'd die if anything happened to you. I'd die . . .'

One nurse grabbed the phone and another dragged Ruth away down the passage, twisting her arm up against her spine in a half-Nelson.

'Sorry about that, Mrs Harrison,' said the nurse left with the telephone. 'She told us she was ringing Mrs Fare. Are you alright?'

'Yes, I'll be alright,' Mum replied weakly, and replaced the receiver.

Ruth stopped struggling.

'Will you *kindly* let go! Thank you.'

She extricated herself from the undignified attention of the charge nurse and walked back to her ward, double chin held high.

Ruth decided against another telephone call and instead set Twinkle to gather the information she required: the date, the very hour if possible, of her mother's return home.

In the intervening days Ruth presented herself as a model patient. The doctors were suspicious at first, one doctor especially. Ruth could easily tell. He kept asking the same questions in different disguises, probing peripheral questions, and studying her intently as she replied. Ruth had nothing to hide and answered all his questions: clearly when she was clear, hesitatingly when she was unsure, always intelligently and at length.

Why didn't she like television? Because it diminished all and everyone it touched – except sport and variety, in neither of which was she interested. Television always disappointed her, even when she watched without expectation. It left her physically and mentally weakened, she felt. Colour was worse than black and white, all the beautiful shades and variations of life processed away, flattened out, steam-ironed into standard forms. It pretended to give you everything and yet left you with nothing; a little, very little retained information and a few clichéd emotions. By supplying its own limiting images it denied her hers. No artist or writer she loved, no work of theirs known or unknown, had ever gained in her eyes from the television treatment. Not for Ruth, no, not for her. For her, television blocked out love; like clouds in front of the sun, it darkened the day.

How did she assess the worth of any individual's life? Hers, for example? Not greatly. No person's life, she meant, was of any great value on its own. In the wider scheme of things the natural loss of a single human life, of many lives even, is no tragedy in itself, the cause more often than not of false public sorrow, of worthless armchair sentimentalism. Floods are natural, aircrashes are natural, murder is natural. Death and decay are part of life. God is the only judge, Jesus the only guide. You can never know if what anyone does is worth anything or not, for there are no yardsticks, no trusty checks and balances: nor right rewards, as she had been so wrongly taught at school. All she could say for sure was that inside, secret from our outside selves, we all know what we are worth. Only we ourselves can assess the value of our own lives before God.

Was there anyone in the village she particularly disliked? No, she did not dislike anyone she actually knew. Feared them perhaps, fantasised about them maybe, but never blamed them personally. Blamed herself. Yet there undoubtedly were certain people in Watham who led dreadful lives, people who did and said horrid things to their wives, to their children, to their friends at work, people she definitely could not say she liked. Humbug she hated more than anything else: the pretence at expertise, knowingness when knowing nothing. And she hated the way men raised themselves on the wreckage of others' lives. Waste of talent she loathed too, the squandering of gifts; good health, good looks, good marriages. Debbie Cornish's husband, Wayne: now there was a bad man, a vicious man. The very devil of a man. He once beat Debbie almost to death with the chain from his motorcycle.

Did she want to have children? Yes. Yes, definitely. But not in her own image. She wanted to be the mother of a good man's children, not of hers alone. 'I want you to be the mother of my children,' Mum had told her Dad had said. She wanted someone to say that to her; she wanted to be the vessel chosen to carry someone else's child, a father's child. The arrogance of such a man would not disturb her; a strong man was what she needed, to balance her own weakness.

Why had she painted? And why had she stopped? For lots of reasons, different reasons at different times. At the beginning simply to occupy the day. She had always liked the mechanics of drawing and painting, the materials and the instruments – and the stillness. Long after the other children at school had poked holes in, scratched and desecrated their tin geometry boxes Ruth's was all but untouched, as good as new. On her fourteenth birthday she had received a special draughtsman's set from Uncle Gordon, in a leather-covered case with snap top, each shiny stainless steel instrument laid in its velveteen place, a whole family of protractors and set squares strapped into the lid. The special joy of a ruler with ivory edges, and an india-ink nib for the compass. Before, and afterwards, there had been the poster paints in stepped rows and the Rowney De Luxe set of oils, thirty-eight different coloured tubes in a plywood case. During her first year of working in oil – two-dimensional studies of individual objects; a cornweave crucifix peppered with dried flowers; Dad's cricket bag; the treadle sewing machine – she had been totally absorbed in the technique, sensually preoccupied with the handling of paint itself. Gradually this had changed and the subjects themselves had come to hold her in thrall, allowing her in the intense delineation of natural life to caress the hands of God. And there was so much else besides, so many feelings within feelings, thoughts within thoughts, more than any doctor could hope to understand.

By the time Twinkle surfaced with the date of Mrs Harrison's return to the Priory, Ruth had an established routine. No one suspected her of thoughts of escape and she had been allowed to take the afternoons to herself, drawing portraits around the wards or wandering with a sketchpad in Dilham's ornamental grounds.

Early on the Wednesday afternoon that Mum was due to be collected from Bath by Mark and Sylvia, Ruth let herself out through a side gate she had seen the nurses use. From Dilham village she took a bus in to Shepton Mallet and from Shepton another on to Eastney, walking to Watham across the fields. The church clock was striking half past four as Ruth climbed the stile into the spinney and approached the verandah. At the foot of the wooden steps she stopped. The windows were dirty, and spiders' webs stretched out from the corners of the glass roof to the creeping shoots of wisteria. Ruth bent to dig with her fingers in the garden path. She pulled up a flint stone and threw it through the studio window. Briskly she mounted the steps, stuck her arm over the jagged edges of the broken pane, and let herself in. She walked on, soiled dancing pumps crunching shattered glass, a single red pompom bobbing at the toe of her left foot, on up the stairs to her mother's bedroom.

The bed. Mum's bed. There was Mum's bed.

Ribbed puce counterpane folded neatly over the polished mahogany footboard. Soft cream blanket tucked tight at the corners, Irish linen sheet turned back at the far side. Four pillows, two-by-two, puffed white. Ivory hair and clothes brushes laid out on the veined marble top of the gentleman's dressing chest. Stagshorn shoehorn. Kidney-shaped dressing table with bevelled glass top, oval mirror, and pleated silk skirt. Matching wastepaper basket and paperhanky box, lace frilled.

Mum's empty slippers on the sheepskin rug, heels broken inwards, once pink tops faded and rubbed smooth.

Ruth closed her eyes. Failing to dam the flow of tears, she pulled the spectacles from her nose and pressed both fists hard into the blind sockets.

Was that really her? Could that possibly have been her?

A smallish girl with thick black hair hanging down her back stood at the half open door: she must have been about five years old, and wore boy's striped pyjamas. The little girl wanted a drink of water, and was about to ask for one. At the last moment, the words on the tip of her tongue, she decided not to speak, and stepped back out of sight behind the bedroom door.

'Naughty, naughty girl,' her father was saying.

Holding her breath she very slowly leant forward to peek into the room.

Her father was seated on the dressing table stool, his burgundy dressing gown untied at the waist and hanging loose to the ground; across his bare knees he supported his wife, balanced on her stomach. The girl's mother giggled, shaking her head as the man pulled up her slip over her bottom. In one hand, high above his head, he waved a woman's hairbrush; with the other he parted her thighs and allowed his fingers to slide slowly up the inside of her leg.

'Who's a naughty girl then?' he crooned.

'Me, me,' her mother mewed.

The little girl's father's hand stroked and played; he lowered his head and licked both buttocks, his saliva glistening in the strip-light from the dressing table mirror. The woman moaned as his finger dug deeper.

'Naughty girl,' he said in a sterner voice and let his other hand fall, the back of the hairbrush descending with a loud report on the flesh of his wife's bottom. 'Naughty, naughty, naughty.'

Slap. Slap! Slap! Louder, harder, faster.

The woman stuffed the silk folds of his dressing gown into her mouth in an attempt to muffle her squeals.

'Mummy,' from behind the door. 'Mummy, I need a glass of water.'

Ruth heard a car approaching down the gravel drive. She dried her eyes, and walking round to her mother's side of the bed extracted a briar rose from her shoulder bag and placed it on the pillow.

When Mrs Harrison shuffled through the green baize door on Sylvia's arm, Ruth was already waiting on the half-landing where the wide stairs turned towards the bedroom.

'Mark, come quickly. Ruth's here!' Sylvia shouted just as Mark strolled into the hall through the dining room door.

Below on the stone flags the three looked up. Above, Ruth stared down. No one moved.

She saw it all. Suddenly, she saw it all: what she had done, why she had come, where she must go. She saw the unguarded flash of terror cross Mum's wounded face. Saw the yellow cartwheel bruises around the old eyes. Saw the swelling on Mum's temple, like a growth, a misplaced goitre. Saw the cross-hatched lines of purple scars crawling over Mum's forehead. Saw the washed white undyed hair and the shaven hairline. She saw that her mother no longer wanted her, no longer needed her, could no longer cope.

Ruth trotted down the stairs.

'Don't worry; Mrs C's cleared everything up. Here, give me your other arm.'

'Have they sent you home too?'

'Not exactly!' Ruth grinned. 'Just see you settled in, then I'm going to All Souls. If they'll have me. Can't risk any more accidents, can we?'

'Dr Cardy knows best. He'll know what to do,' Mrs Harrison replied.

They looked long into each other's faces, and smiled. Ruth rubbed her head against her mother's shoulder and squeezed the limp hand.

'You've done all you can, Mum. It's up to me now. I'm on my own now,' she added quietly, almost to herself.

Sylvia took charge thereafter. Having put Mrs Harrison to bed she rang the hospital to assure them Ruth would be returned the next day, either to Dilham or All Souls. They dined on quiche and ratatouille, brought with them from Bradfield St Clare; after supper they took their mugs of cocoa upstairs to Dad's study, close enough to hear Mum call. Mark sat himself at the desk and thumbed through his father's game books stacked on a shelf above the radiogram, leaving Sylvia, by implication, to deal with Ruth.

'I'm glad you realise it's impossible to stay here. We wanted your mother to come home with us, but she wouldn't hear of it.' Sylvia paused. 'She is a bit frightened of you, I'm afraid. Knows you didn't really mean any harm. We all do, don't we, Mark?'

'Of course,' he muttered, without looking up.

'Never mind. It's over now. The important thing's to make sure nothing like this happens again.'

'How? Other than by locking me up!'

'We did think of that, to be honest. It just . . .'

Mark interrupted her, furiously.

'*We* did nothing of the sort. You and your *mother* did. Ruthie, I'd never let them commit you. Word of honour. When you're better you can come back home. Promise. It's for your own good, you know that.'

'Yes, Marky, I know. I've always known.'

The following day Mark and Ruth took a train to London, an early train so Mark could deliver his sister to All Souls without being too late at work. He hired a taxi all the way east from Paddington Station. Ruth loved taxis. Whenever she climbed into a London cab, which was not very often, she felt bubbles of anticipation burst inside her tummy – a long-term legacy from Dad's Christmas trips to the pantomime. And it *was* exciting, in its way, to be returning to All Souls.

Ruth remembered how unhappy she had been to leave last time. She pictured the welcoming smile on Salma's dark face; looked forward to the daily swim at York Hall Baths, to the kids playing on the parabola diving tower. Boys launching their angular bodies fearlessly head first from the ten-metre board, thinking they could dive – and so they could, after their own fashion, with the accompanying chorus of jeers and honey-pots and laughter. The Hans Andersen turrets of St Pancras Station passed by the windows of the taxi. Further on they came to the Angel, The Latimer Seamen's Mission, Hackney Christian Science Hostel, the Central Foundation School of Needlework, Hoxton Tabernacle, St Leonard's Shoreditch, the Quaker Hospital for Tropical Diseases, Bethnal Green Bingo Hall. So many ports of refuge. Surely there had to be one for her too, somewhere? There had to be: there was no going back, not this time.

Ruth ran from the taxi trailing two coats over her arm, tripped and almost fell. Undaunted, she continued on up the steps and pushed eagerly through the glass door.

'I'm here!'

Mark followed her in. He put her bags down by the desk, and rebuttoned the jacket of his summer suit.

'Must rush I'm afraid. Cab's waiting. I'll be in touch.'

He pecked her cheek, and stepped away.

'Marky! There's no need to run away like that. You've got to believe. You do, don't you?'

'Of course I do. I'm late for work, that's all. 'Bye for now. Take care.'

He kissed her again and squeezed her hand. He looked as if he wanted to say something, still holding his sister's fingers.

'Yes?'

'Nothing,' he replied, turned and walked to the door.

'Give my love to Sylvia,' she called after him. 'And thank you. *Thank you.*'

At the porch he waved, and was gone.

Too stupid, she kept telling herself, to have expected everything to be the same. It couldn't be: she had beaten Mum over the head with the dustpan-brush. How could they possibly understand? They were bound to put her in the Muriel Kenny Ward, up on the first floor at the end of the passage.

'Where're you going?' the charge nurse asked through his watching glass door.

'For a walk in the Park.'

'Not now you aren't. There's no one free to go with you.'

Patience. She must be patient. It wasn't their fault, they didn't know who she was. If only Dr Cardy wasn't away. A hip operation. How long did that take? Months, she imagined. There was no one she knew in Cavell Ward, they said. She would not believe them, and begged to be taken down to see for herself.

The new curtains looked nice – pink stripes.

Twelve o'clock at last, and Salma arrived on duty, spick and span as ever, a diminutive figure clattering down the ward on illegally high-heeled shoes.

'Salma! I'm so pleased to see you. They've put me in the wrong ward.'

The truth. Salma's dark eyes never lie; the black pupils and dusty whites of her Eastern eyes can't lie.

'No? Is this where I'm meant to be?'

Salma is thinking of Mum, I can see it; and wondering how anyone can do such a thing. Her faith in me gone, withered away.

'Yes. For the time being. Is there anything I can get you?' Salma asked.

Ruth dropped onto her bed. She buried her face in the pillow and covered her head with her hands. Salma leant over and patted Ruth's rigid shoulders, stroked her back.

'Now-now, don't take on so. We've got to find out what the trouble is. Be a good girl now.'

Go away! Go away! For the Lord Jesus Christ's sake leave me in peace. Why don't you all leave me in peace? I can't, I'm too tired. I just want to be left alone. What is it you expect from me? Nothing to give. There's nothing there. I've told you so many times: I'm no good, not worth bothering about. However hard I try everything always goes wrong, always will. You must give up, go away, let me be.

Salma grimaced, her heart again touched by the special agony of Ruth's wordless wail.

'Don't. Please,' she whispered.

At nine-thirty the next morning, while the rest of the ward was at remedials, Ruth was taken down to Dr Tobias. It was a long session, nearly two hours, the first of many – as many as might prove necessary. Necessary for what, she had asked? To wean her from her drugs, he seemed to be saying. What about the chemical imbalance? A turn of phrase – *façon de parler*, were his actual words – with no real meaning. Her chemical imbalance, after all these years, it didn't mean anything? No, that wasn't possible: she was ill, had been for fifteen years. The chemistry of mind and body, the balance between the two, was always changing, he said. Drugs may once have been the solution, may again be, but first they had to help her find her natural space. Did Dr Cardy know about this? Dr Cardy knew about everything at All Souls. Well . . . yes, it did make sense. It was what she had been saying all along, that she must learn to trust in herself as well as in God. Dr Tobias didn't seem too keen on God. He'd learn! She'd teach him to love God and he'd teach her to love herself. That's a fair deal.

'How's the crow today?'

What!

Ruth raised her head. Sitting on the next bed, long fishnet-stockinged legs elegantly crossed, was a woman in her late thirties. She was smoking a cigarette, her lips pursed, one eye closed against the smoke.

'Sorry, what did you say?' Ruth asked.

'Dr Tobias, is he on form today? Never mind. I'm Brigit Crighton. You weren't up to introductions yesterday. Ruth Who are you?'

'Harrison. I've . . .'

'I know some Harrisons. In Putney. Any relation?'

'Might be. We're a bit cut off down in Somerset. It might be my cousin. Luke's his name. I'm not sure what his wife's called.'

Brigit Crighton did not reply. Her heavily powdered face tensed, and the smudged cupid's bow of her painted lips trembled.

'What are your friends' names?' Ruth asked, to break the silence.

'I can't remember. They're not my friends, they're my husband's. He's turned them all against me. Told everyone I'm stark raving mad. You don't think I'm mad, do you?'

'I think you're beautiful, Brigit. You look like Joan Crawford, my Dad's pin-up. Perhaps I could draw you?'

'*Lady* Brigit if you please. And *Mister* Nicholas Crighton. Would you believe, he never forgave me that? Bloody fool. Correction: the stupidest man I've ever met in my life. Christ, what difference does it make? Of course you can call me Brigit, we're going to be friends. Are you good at drawing? I'm *sure* you are.'

She smiled warmly. Ruth smiled back, ridiculously relieved to have made a friend.

They chatted till lunchtime, Ruth struggling to make sense of it all; Brigit talked so fast, and did not always mean what she said. It was difficult to tell when she was being sarcastic, when serious.

In the afternoon – every weekday afternoon, Ruth was soon to learn – the whole ward met in the games room for group therapy. There was Gillian, a dark-haired girl not yet twenty-one, with a heart tattooed on the bridge of her nose; the melancholy Christine; another Brigit – a West Indian who went berserk at least twice a week; old Mrs Callanan, who seldom spoke; Wendy, the ward joker; Ruth's Brigit; and Ruth herself. The tubular steel stacking chairs with ragged canvas seats were ranged in a semi-circle facing a therapist Ruth had not met before. Dr Tobias wandered in and out, standing at the back bouncing a table tennis ball on the floor and interjecting an occasional question of his own. Dr Tobias wore jeans and a crewneck sweater with 'I'm Trev Fly Me' emblazoned across his hunched shoulders. He had given up smoking and cease-

lessly sucked Polo mints. Dr Tobias' presence made the skin
prickle on the back of Ruth's neck.

'You were somewhat bossy at therapy yesterday,' he said the
next day at their morning session.

Oh no! Was I?

'I wasn't.'

'No?'

'No.'

'What were you then?'

'I was trying to be helpful. The doctor lady didn't get what
Brigit was saying. I tried to help, that's all.'

Have I done wrong? What have I done wrong? He won't look
me in the face. Tell me! Please tell me and I won't do it again. I
can't bear these silences. He's so slow. What's he writing?
Another Polo.

'Like a mint?' he offered.

Ruth laughed and a spark of surprise flamed behind Dr
Tobias' tinted spectacles.

'Why are you laughing?'

'At you,' she replied.

He raised his eyebrows, and sucked.

'Tell me, Ruth, why did you say all those things to Gillian?
You've only just met her. How do you know she doesn't know
how to love? Heart on nose, ummm?'

He's joking. Gillian hates everyone. Her own children, she
said so. He must be joking. I won't reply.

'You concentrate on yourself, young woman; and leave the
others to me. Understand? Now, this is your fourth visit to All
Souls, isn't it? What seems to go wrong?'

It all became worse, very much worse, before things slowly
started to improve. There were times during those ten weeks in
the Muriel Kenny Ward when she was so confused in thought
and feeling that she failed to recognise anything familiar about
herself at all, when she feared that she might never find the
bridge back into her own mind, to Ruth. She tried so hard, and
it always went wrong. At group meetings the other patients
complained about her, said she wanted everything her own
way, said she answered all the questions before anyone else had
a chance. Yet when she didn't say anything the sessions disinte-

grated and Christine would be allowed to ramble on about macrobiotic cabbage, or Brigit lectured them on the National Front, ordered them to 'stand up and be counted' – and they did, they all did. It was heart-breaking. If she held her peace, Dr Tobias accused her of sabotage; if she spoke her mind, Gillian swore at her. In all those weeks Mrs Callanan uttered once only: one afternoon, while Ruth was talking, she shouted out 'God stinks' and spat on the floor. Even Brigit laughed at that, both Brigits did. Ruth told them the truth and they all laughed. What more could she do? How could she live in the world if no one let her in?

Week by week they took away more of her pills until she was left with one miserly dose of thyroxine for a thyroid deficiency Dr Tobias had diagnosed. Such a tyrant. A cold unloving man, a stranger to mercy, God forgive him. God will; God forgives us all.

If only Dr Cardy had been there to protect her from this pointless suffering. He knew the truth.

Dr Tobias kept telling her she was consumed with anger, raging, rioting with an unquenched internal anger.

A virgin at thirty-two. Had she no right to be angry? Of course she had: her golden years laid waste, a wilderness. Look what she had become. Her body felt, smelt, of decay: putrid flesh flapping at ugly thighs as she stumbled to the grave. Hair had started to grow on her back, in the sweat hollows between her shoulder blades – she could see it in the washroom mirror. Black bristles like a sea urchin's tentacles sprouted at her ears and threatened her chin. And between her legs, at her Venus mount? A tight curly bush guarding the gates of love? Oh no! The sparse puppy fur of early puberty, nothing more.

No man worthy of the name would deign to touch so gross a creature: of this, if nothing else, there could be no doubt.

They encouraged her to express an anger she did not truly feel, did not fully trust, Ruth sometimes felt. Yet, what other explanation could there be? She must be angry with somebody or something. How else could she have done what she did? How else could she have been driven to take it out on Mum?

No!

No, it couldn't be that. Whatever Dr Tobias said it couldn't be Mum. It was Conor, or Mark or Robin. Twinkle perhaps. Dad even. Dr Cardy and his useless optimism. The exams. Her dream of being an artist. That dreadful Andy Heath. All of this, and all of them were to blame. Anyone but Mum. She loved Mum. Mum was her life-line.

For several weeks, in letters and telephone calls, Ruth hurled abuse across the face of the earth. She cut out Mrs Sayers's tongue in Bradfield St Clare; she castrated Uncle Gordon on his boat in the Bay of Toulon; she burnt Conor's Exeter home to the ground. And to Vancouver she wrote:

Dear Gray,
I had this dream at 5.30 am.
We were in a hotel bedroom. You'd taken me out from hospital. It was night and we were dressed. You were sweet.
Suddenly you got up from the bed and went spare 'What the hell did you hurt me like that for? God it isn't true'
I shouted 'Because it needed saying and the only two people who've ever known you intimately have said these things. But they don't matter'
You were on the floor. I took your face in my hands very tenderly.
Your eyes went little and ugly. I kissed you gently on the forehead and said calmly 'Gray, I don't want you'. You said about a woman getting pleasure and a man none. I said 'Of course. But with my body, I thee worship'
You took me into the street then. You put both hands on my shoulders and said 'I don't know if I should wait till you're sound'
I said 'When are you going to start? You may get no pleasure but give me pleasure'. You very gently chewed my throat.
It was exquisite.
Then you gave up. So I bit your neck several times.
Then you kissed me full on the mouth. I couldn't respond. You opened my mouth with your tongue and very violently whirled mine around. Then you got

impatient. I said 'Remember what we said about patience'. You paced up the narrow street and leaned against the wall.

The street was lit. A beautiful fair child came running down the pavement and fell crack on his head. He got up swearing. On the pavement was a thin pool of blood.

A girl from All Souls said 'Ruth, it's nearly six. Are you coming in to our chamber concert?'

You went down some steps ahead of me.

'Didn't you find it exquisite?' you asked.

'It was like being strangled'

(Here she had left a line blank on the ruled-off notepaper.)

It is all suffering. That is the way, the truth and the life.

It will get better in certain ways but it will never get better.

That is what being loved by God means. And that is what I am. And all I want to be. The pain is so terrible, Gray, that I can do nothing when I am in its throes. I cannot make a life of my own, I am not physically capable. I suffer for Christ. He always looks after me. I do not seek further than the moment. The pain is too great, beyond description.

Did I tell you about the dark night of the soul? I think I'm in for it again. God leads you out of your depth in total darkness until He draws you completely to Himself. The light of Him naked is hard to bear.

Please commit yourself more and more. Very simply. Trust. I love you.

                                        Ruth

(The signature was followed by a kiss, a crucifix and a heart, all three in hieroglyphs.)

There were certain things about the Tobias regime at All Souls which made perfect sense to Ruth. She liked, for example, his willingness to listen; more than willingness, it was a genuine interest in what she had to say. With Dr Cardy it was always she who had asked the questions, he who had provided the answers; with Dr Tobias everything was the other way round. She could clearly see the point; also, in talking about private things, dreams and memories. At one session she told him about the Graham dream, and asked if he understood what she meant.

'No,' he had replied.

'No? But you *must!*'

'No. *You* must.'

Ruth had liked that.

What she didn't like was his refusal to become a friend. But I'm not your friend, he would always say, I'm your doctor.

For male friendship Ruth turned instead to Neil Skinner, a boy in the lower men's ward. She and Brigit and Neil soon formed a kind of gang in their free hours, supporting each other through times of crisis. It was an unlikely partnership: Brigit, tall and angular and elegant, Ruth, broad and strong, Neil, bow-legged and wiry, a streetwise Londoner. They developed a close friendship though, and were often to be seen strolling up and down the hall, arms tightly linked; or sitting squashed close together on the settee at Sunday night television. Their physical contact was always so intense and personal, as though courage could pass from one to the other by touch. However many times Ruth, Brigit and Neil gave up hope for themselves, they never despaired for each other.

Brigit needed Ruth most, as it happened, on returning to the hospital after a brief supervised visit home. It was a much talked-about visit, hard-earned by three weeks best behaviour, a golden opportunity to prove herself, Dr Tobias had called it. Brigit often spoke of her Chelsea house, the first real home of her own, purchased a year before with the divorce money. ('Beastly judge didn't actually *say* I was barmy, merely implied it,' she used to say, in a clatter of cocktail party laughter.) With all the talk Brigit's house had taken shape in Ruth's mind. Brigit's house had a cobalt-blue door with vertical letter-box and laurel-leaf knocker, no bell. The front room curtains were never drawn – Ruth was not sure they could be – and a light was always on inside, usually the table lamp (a colourful Chinese vase with mottled shade). There was a duet stand, a Madame

Recamier chaise longue, fashion prints on the walls, four kelim rugs, and French windows leading down a spiral staircase to the back garden. These features of the house were more or less constant, the rest changed with Ruth's mood. Occasionally there was a small room at the top of the house with a view of the River Thames from its dormer window, and a pine table at which Ruth sometimes painted in the evening after work.

'Bitch, bitch, bitch, bitch . . .' Brigit endlessly mouthed, standing at the end of her bed, thin fingers gripping the paint-chipped rail. Her smart fawn skirt was soiled, twisted askew, and a bruise flushed purple at the side of her face. Ruth guided her friend to the bedside chair. ' . . . bitch, bitch, bitch . . .'

'Who? What happened? Bri, speak to me. What's happened?'

Brigit sat down, crossed her legs and lit a cigarette. She shrugged.

'Agent provocateur. A woman of my experience should've known better. Caught napping there, I'm afraid, Ruth love.' She sniffed. 'No point in trying to stop her, she'd've called up reinforcements to work me over, like last time. I sat on the stairs and let her get on with it. Showed my maturity there at least.'

'Oh Bri, how awful. Who?'

'Nurse McIntyre. Been nobbled by the NF, see. She went berserk as soon as I opened the door. Smashed every window in the place. And pissed on the kitchen floor for good measure.'

Brigit paused for effect. Ruth looked away, avoiding her eye.

'Clever bitch has already framed me. Told the crow I did it myself. I ask you, why on earth would I break my own windows? It's a ludicrous accusation, it really is. Of course he believes McIntyre's story. Paranoid liar they've got me down as. Labelled for life, I am. Nothing I can possibly do about it.'

Brigit sniggered. Ruth put a protective arm about her friend's shoulders, kneeling down at her side. It wasn't true, Ruth knew it wasn't true. Brigit had done the same kind of thing before, she admitted so herself, had thrown bricks through her own windows and sprayed National Front slogans across the wall.

If only I could do something to help. Perhaps, when we're both ready to go home, perhaps if Bri and I could live together, loving and caring for each other, she wouldn't need to do these things? Nothing's impossible. And it would be my home too, in a way. Bri wouldn't do it to *my* home, I'm sure. It might work. It really might.

I'm going to give it a try! Oh I am, I am! Bri, dear Bri, it's going to be alright.

It's worse than usual, I know, up here in the Muriel Kenny. But we'll manage. We will. I promise.

2

Days came and went, taking with them the last of summer. Rain fell on the games room's corrugated roof where Ruth escaped in the evenings to nurture her dreams of the Chelsea life to come, guarding her hopes till Brigit was well enough to think of a real future.

Retaliation was all Brigit could talk of at first, of her crusade to unite the working man with the aristocracy, together to fight the evils of fascism. It was a mistake, she insisted, a cleverly conceived political red herring to present it all as a war between left and right, between the have-nothings and the have-everythings; the real battle, the one those double-dealing fat-cats in power really feared was the battle against the middle, the true steel of the united ends annihilating the mushy middle. The trouble was, if Ruth understood her friend correctly, that the ruling middle-class got up to all sorts of dirty tricks in order to prevent this happening, the National Front being one of the foulest of these tricks – an overtly anti-democratic movement which the working class and the upper class each suspected the other of being behind when in actual fact it was a diversion funded by the political élite themselves, the underground Lab-Con-Lib alliance.

'Why do you imagine they picked on me? Because they thought I'd automatically blame the workers. Middle class bigots like my *dear* husband think they've got the likes of me taped. Huh! Got another think coming. Their little plan back-fired. Blew up in their grubby little faces.'

'How exactly?'

'Sorry, sweetie, forgot I was talking to a political ostrich. It's had precisely the opposite effect. Can't you see, the workers know I'm on their side now. We're allies. The enemy is without.'

'What are you going to do?'

'Got to get out of this place first. Not going to be all that easy, I'm afraid. They'll want to keep me *hors de combat* for as long as they can. I can't actually see the answer yet. I'm working on it, though. Don't worry, I'll get us out of here somehow.'

In a comradely gesture, Brigit chucked Ruth under the chin. At least she thinks of us as 'us', Ruth consoled herself. It was a start.

All the same, as whole weeks disappeared into the trough of hospital routine and Ruth came no closer to reserving a future for herself, her hopes faltered. Feeling a little better made the waiting worse. Freed from obsessive worry she had more time to think. She was no longer so upset by the failure of group therapy meetings to follow the direction she might consider most beneficial. There was no need, she realised, to seek tangible proof of progress the whole time; life need not necessarily be seen as a succession of material achievements, as a pyramid of unlimitable attainment up which you climb. On, on up the steep sides of the pyramid, never resting, looking neither up nor down, nor out over the soft dunes, only ahead to the next sweat-spattered step. Till you are too tired to continue and fall to your knees on the hard stone; only then, when you know it is impossible to progress another inch do you dare admit that each new level of achievement, each step up, was exactly like the last, that you might as well have been quietly clambering down for all the difference it would have made to your finished life. Rest, she told herself; you have struggled enough, and to no avail. Rest was what she wanted, if only she could find a place to lay her head.

Please God, my dear, great, good Goddi, give Bri a bit of a hand, won't you? I know she hasn't asked for your help, but she thinks you're on the other side, you see.

You didn't come to judge the world but to save it. Save Bri: forgive her for she knows not what she does.

You'd be saving two birds with one stone. Two in the hand and none in the bush!

Sorry, I didn't mean to be funny. It slipped out. It's that

Wendy, she never stops cracking jokes and I've caught the habit. Seriously though, it would be a great help to me if you could see your way to nudging Bri in the right direction. That's all. Bless you, Goddi. Bless you.

The first time Ruth mentioned her idea to Brigit was one Sunday morning when Dr Tobias had allowed them down to the Cheshire Street junk market.

From a stall at the mouth of a fire-blackened warehouse Brigit extracted a lustre teapot.

'How much is this?' she asked.

'Fiver.'

'Five pounds? Can't be!'

'Tell you what. Three quid and a kiss. Can't be fairer than that, can I, duckie?'

Brigit laughed. She looked wonderful, so relaxed and confident.

'Two pounds and it's a deal,' she replied, and offered him her cheek.

Ignoring the cheek, the stallholder gave her a smacking kiss on the lips.

'That's alright, darlin'. Keep yer money, tea's on me. Be good,' he shouted after them. 'But if you wanter be bad, I'll be 'appy to oblige.'

They walked on down the cobbled street, arms linked.

'You're *such* a friend, Ruthie. I love it with you.'

'Me too. It's fun here, isn't it? Oh do look. Look! Puppies! I don't believe it.'

They had reached Sclater Street, home of the East End Livestock Market, a chaotic jumble of squeaking, squawking, barking stalls: hamsters, kittens, tortoises, puppies, canaries, parrots, tropical fish, mina birds, white mice, snakes, pigeons, and a man pulling ferrets out of his trousers.

'Oh!' Brigit shrieked, eyes popping. 'I say, *do* be careful!'

Ruth was peering into a large cardboard box at the other side of the road. 'Over here, Bri, quick!'

In a bed of shredded paper at the bottom of the box three labrador puppies ragged and romped, falling over their own outsized feet and crashing into the sides of the box.

'We always had labs at home. Marvellous companions,

almost human. *Don't*. Don't touch them, they're riddled with disease, poor brutes.'

'They aren't. Are they?' Ruth queried. 'How can you tell? They look perfect to me.'

'Buy a goldfish. Can't go wrong with fish. Come on.' Brigit tugged at the hood of Ruth's duffel coat, pulling her away from the smooth talk of the barely-teenage boy in charge of the puppies. 'Can't trust their breeding,' she added. 'Grow up with tails curling above their backsides.'

Ruth laughed. Quite right, they probably would: 'Like question marks. Who's my father?'

Underneath the railway bridge they bought themselves paper cups of coffee at a hot-dog stand. Was this the moment to share the dream? Ruth turned to look at her friend, leaning against the damp brick, both hands holding the red Coca-Cola cup of coffee which she blew to cool, intelligent green eyes darting from spot to spot in the market crowd. Yes, why not?

'Bri. Could I ask you something?'

'Fire away.'

'You will say if it's not possible, won't you? You mustn't say yes just to please me.'

'Good God, no. I'm in the business of pleasing myself, didn't you know? Come on, out with it.'

'It's just an idea. We get on so well, I just wondered if we could live together when we're better?'

'Ruth really, you are a dope. As if I didn't know? You've been planning this for weeks. Come on, admit it.'

'You aren't angry, are you?'

'Of course I bloody am. Plotting behind my back. At least you don't deny it. Proves something, I suppose.'

'I'm not plotting, I promise. It was just a dream. A silly dream.'

The thin figure of Brigit in a rakishly cut tweed suit. Ruth a whole head shorter, looking as though she might fall to her knees at her friend's feet. Wastepaper bowling along the pavement in the wind.

'Cheer up. I think it's a wonderful idea,' Brigit said, and kissed Ruth on the forehead. 'I'd love you to live with me.'

It was, they agreed, best to keep the plan to themselves – for safety's sake. At first they didn't even tell Neil.

'The crow's got his beady eye on Neil,' Brigit claimed. 'Safer if he's nothing to confess.'

Whenever the two of them were alone though, they talked insatiably of the things they would do together, of the life they would lead. Ruth had heard from Mrs Fitzgerald about an art history course at the Victoria and Albert Museum and they planned to enrol in the spring.

'Splendid. We'll lunch at that new Brasserie in the Brompton Road. At the bar,' Brigit envisaged.

Ruth could hardly wait: a home in London, the impossible come true. And the people Brigit talked about all sounded so fascinating. She planned to give at least one dinner party a week, with six guests, and two wines, at the round table in the kitchen.

'No one gives formal dinners these days. Personally I have the Perrier on the table,' Brigit assured.

Brigit's brother, Plumpton, was already Ruth's favourite. He was unmarried, and ran the family chain of chemist shops from a secluded retreat in Herefordshire. Ruth intended to call him Christopher, his other name.

'Plumpton's a hoot. You'll love him,' Brigit promised.

There was a doctor friend of Brigit's who sounded nice too, and a merchant banker she had nearly married, and a Persian – Iranians they preferred to be called, apparently – she had met skiing in Gstaad. Then there was Georgie Phelps, one-time amateur rackets champion, who drank a little too much but never let it show. A cousin at the Ministry of Agriculture and Fisheries would do to make up numbers if they were short; and Douglas Jarrold would soon be back from his stint in Northern Ireland.

'Needs watching, mind you. Quite the ladies' man,' Brigit warned.

'Your cousin?'

'Christ, no. Douglas.'

Not all their talk was social; there was a serious side to it as well, since each planned to support the other in their work, Ruth in Brigit's determination to create a political platform for herself, and Brigit in Ruth's projected career as a church muralist. They also spoke openly about their illnesses.

'It's true. My breaking up the house is a mad sort of reaction to Nicholas leaving. I can't tell you how lonely I feel sometimes. And you? Why do you bash furniture?'

'Dr Tobias says it's anger. I don't know. I think I was probably trying to get away. If nothing was left there'd be no reason to stay, would there?'

'And your mother?'

'The same, I think. When you meet her you'll see why I love Mum so much. She's got this incredible serenity. She seems above it all. Untouchable.'

'Why do you want to come to me then? Why not home to your mother?'

'Because you're my Naomi.'

It had started as a game, this drawing of Biblical parallels, a game which for Ruth at least had the ring of truth.

'Wash thyself,' Naomi told her, 'and anoint thee, and put thy raiment upon thee, and get thee down to the floor.' To Boaz Ruth must go, to Naomi's cousin. 'And uncover his feet, and lay thee down.'

Later they were married: the Moabite and the Israelite, the outcast and the priest, the woman and the man.

Me too, Goddi. Me too.

'A new commandment I give unto you, that ye love one another; as I loved you, that ye also love one another.'

Amen to that, I say.

I do, Goddi. I've always tried to, you know that.

On the day before Neil was due to be discharged Brigit and Ruth took him out for a farewell tea in Victoria Park, at the refreshment kiosk underneath the bandstand. The miserable grey of the sky reflected their mood. Neil, his ginger crew-cut furrowed by the November breeze, stared across the grass at a gypsy exercising his pony: round and round the dappled pony galloped at the end of a rope. Next to Neil, Bri's fingers paddled in the millimetre-deep pools of rainwater on the metal table top, creating rivers and lakes and, through the hole in the centre, a Niagara Falls. Ruth was gazing at Neil gazing at the gypsy, and thinking how fond she was of him. She remembered the time she had lain on top of him to quell one of his trembling fits, her full weight bearing down on Neil's small frame, head pressed to his chest, hands blindfolding his eyes. 'You've got it beat. You've got it beat,' she had repeated, echoing his own words; an affirmation, she had hoped. Tomorrow he'd be gone, to a new rehabilitation home in Poole. 'Third time lucky,' he often said. Was it luck one needed? Ruth saw him rub the palms of his hands down the lapels of his leather jacket, and wondered.

'It honestly doesn't matter about the spelling,' she said. 'You will write? Promise?'

'Yeh, I'll write. I don't mind any more. Not with friends.'

'Not with anyone, Neil. It doesn't matter what people think of you. Just don't be tempted.'

'Right on. I've learned my lesson this time. Pride before a fall, eh?'

'Right on,' Ruth confirmed, and put out her hand, palm upwards, to receive the ritual Harlem slap Neil had taught her to expect.

'You can come and stay with us when you're in town, if you like,' Brigit said, casually revealing their secret.

Ruth beamed, and started to explain: 'You see, us two're going to live together. In Glebe Place. There'll be a bed for you anytime. Won't there, Bri?'

'Open house, my dear. Alcoholics anonymous.'

'Piss off! Another cuppa?'

'Yes, please,' Brigit and Ruth chimed in together.

They sat chatting in Victoria Park until almost five, before hurrying back to All Souls for their evening meal.

A major outcome of Ruth's continued improvement, apart from her removal downstairs to the Cavell Ward, was her mother's surprise visit: at midday on the Saturday after Neil's departure.

Ruth couldn't believe her eyes. Was it her? A wave, and that familiar chicken-like shake of the head. It was. It really was.

'Mum!'

'Ruthiemoo.'

They hugged. Pulled away. Laughed in each other's faces. And hugged again.

'Why didn't you warn me? I look such a mess.'

'No, you don't, you look lovely, dear.'

'Did they say you could come?'

'Asked me. Rang me up, didn't they?'

'Who did? You spoke to Dr Tobias?'

'Nice young man he sounded. Awfully polite.'

'Dr Tobias? Honestly, Mum! He thinks you're a monster. He *does*.'

'Couldn't have been him who rang then, could it?'

They laughed again, snorting and hooting.

'Sorry,' Mrs Harrison said to the ward in general, and to the nearest nurse. 'I'm Ruth's mother.'

'We rather gathered that,' the nurse replied. 'Carry on, don't mind us.'

They sat together on Ruth's bed and talked non-stop till lunch, all through lunch too which they took on their own in the games room. Afterwards they went for a walk and Ruth showed Mum the Park, the Baths and the Museum, all the places she had written about in her letters, forgetting for the moment that her mother had seen it all before.

'You must introduce me to Neil,' Mum suggested.

'Neil's not here.'

'What a pity. Next time.'

'No, he's gone for good. To a Home in Dorset.'

'I thought you said he lived in Deptford?'

'A Home, not home.'

'Oh, I see. Can't be helped.'

'Brigit's been longing to meet you. You'll adore her; she's the best friend I've ever had. I hope . . .'

'I thought we might go to the zoo next weekend,' Mum interrupted. 'Would you like that? I'd come up in the car.'

'You mean, you're coming again?'

'Don't you want me to?'

'Of course I do. It's all I've ever wanted. I just didn't think *they* wanted it.'

'Why ever not? Oh, you mean all that. Goodness no, I've completely recovered. I'm fine now.'

At the zoo in Regent's Park next weekend, Mrs Harrison and Ruth rushed from the penguin pool to the rhinoceros house and back to the sea-lions in a vain attempt to catch all the animals at feeding time. The penguins were the funniest, flip-flapping in convoy up and down the curved slipways and diving to chase dead fish. The sea-lions never stopped barking even as they ate: very rude, Mum pointed out, talking with their mouths full. It was a cold day and they spent a mesmerised hour in the tropical heat of the reptile house, searching for camouflaged lizards amongst the sand and stones, and jumping back in shock when they suddenly spotted the creatures in front of their noses, captive behind the glass. Snakes shed their skins, miniature turtles practised swimming, and the alligators chewed the ends of each others' tails.

Whenever and wherever they were away on holiday one of Dad's first concerns had always been to locate the nearest zoo. Dad was good at clicking his tongue and sucking his teeth until an idle ape ambled over for a chat. Other children, whole families in fact, used to follow Dad around zoos applauding his tricks and begging him to make another hippopotamus yawn, the hyena laugh again, a vulture spread his wings, the giraffes dance the cha-cha. The one thing Dad had never been able to do was halt the polar bear's ceaseless pacing of his rocky gaol. The great creamy-white creature still padded, remorselessly, from end to end: around a boulder at the top, along the side of his pool and up onto his big hind legs at the wall, raising his paws, stretching his neck, rolling his red eyes, opening his mouth in a silent growl and twisting back to begin another circuit. Only at feeding time did the bear pause, and plunged into the water after an apple or a hunk of raw meat. What could you do? On Christmas Day Cindy once presented them with eight puppies and Ruth had spent the rest of the holidays guarding the half-blind runt of the litter, guiding him towards a full teat of milk, holding back his greedy brothers and sisters.

Ruth felt confused. Before seeing her mother again she had been able to plot her future quite clearly, had mapped out for herself a careful route from the Muriel Kenny to the Cavell Ward, from All Souls to the half-way hostel in Woolwich and from the hostel, hopefully, to Glebe Place. There was no place for Mum in her present plans, only in the far-off future. Had she made some dreadful mistake, she asked Dr Tobias? What had she done wrong? No, she was doing splendidly, he promised, it was simply a question of adjustment, of fine tuning, like the engine of a racing car. Ruth had never before thought of her body as a racing car. It didn't seem to help much. A radio, then, he suggested. Like turning from programme to programme on a radio, and from long wave to medium wave to VHF. Mum was a very high frequency station on which there was continuous interference; they must find out where the fault lay, in reception or transmission, and correct it. Honestly! What a loony idea. No two human beings could be on a closer wavelength than she and Mum. They understood each other so well there was scarcely need for speech. The trouble with Dr Tobias was that he failed to separate love from the rest of human emotions. He put love alongside pain and anger. He missed the point; sadly, he always misses the point. Love – the love of God – transcends life. Love assuages pain, forgives anger. Dr Tobias' trouble is that he has no faith.

'You're not at all frightened of me any more, are you?'

It was a couple of weekends later. They were sitting in the Beefeater Lounge, a room in Mum's hotel reserved for residents in the afternoon and for functions in the evening.

'I never was. Not of you. I was frightened of dying.'

'Mum!'

'I know. But I was.'

'Why?'

'Because of what Dad would say, mainly.'

'If I'd killed you?'

'He'd've blamed me. Wouldn't he?'

Ruth thought about this, and bit into a macaroon.

'Close your mouth, there's a dear.'

'Bri says you taste more with your mouth open.'

Mum laughed. 'Well, she was joking.'

'You think Dad would've blamed you for letting me get into such a state?' Mum nodded, and Ruth helped herself to another macaroon. 'Then he doesn't understand either.'

'I doubt if men ever do. My, look at the time. We'd better be off. Not well enough for a function yet, are we dear?'

The joy of her mother's company was almost too much for Ruth: she nearly cried. What was the point of their being apart, of denying herself all this? The love, the fun, the understanding. Of denying it Mum too. For the sake of what? Of learning to be like everyone else: in control, wise to the world, faithless?

To exorcise the agony, that was the real point. The one valid point.

At the Wallace Collection on another occasion, sitting on an upholstered bench in the bay window, they discussed the hostel.

'Why not give it a try? It mightn't be that bad,' Mum suggested.

'Woolwich, though. Sounds so depressing.'

'Not far from Deptford.'

'Really?'

'Make you appreciate home!'

They squeezed hands; Ruth continued to fiddle with the rings on her mother's fingers. 'Do I have to?'

'Perhaps they'd take you to have a look first.'

'I could ask, I suppose. Wouldn't make much difference, they've already made up their minds.'

'It's not up to them,' Mum replied, with a touch of anger in her voice. '*I'm* your mother.'

They got up and wandered through into an upstairs gallery.

'There's a clown. Look, Mum. Peeping round the column.'

'So gay.'

'You do like Bri?'

'Of course I do, darling. She's a character. Sweet of her to invite you to stay.'

'I might learn to type. It's ever so easy to get a job in London if you can type. And it'd be a help to Bri.'

'I don't think much of that picture. He's got the nose all wrong.'

'Don't say that. Maybe it's meant to be wrong.'

'I wish you'd start to paint again.'

'I might. Perhaps when I'm back home.'

'That'll be nice.'

Yes, it will. It'll be lovely. Not having to worry what anyone thinks any more. I can hardly wait. All the endless explaining. What do I mean by this, how do I react to that, where do I place the other? As if there's an answer to everything. There isn't. It begins as it ends, with God.

'Thank you, thank you,' Ruth whispered when she and Mum

separated on the steps of All Souls at the close of another weekend together.

'Thank *you*, Ruthiemoo.'

Dr Tobias himself suggested a preparatory visit to the Glen Creran Hostel in Woolwich. Ruth could travel down by train with Salma after tea one afternoon, he said, meet Mr and Mrs Macnair-Stuart, spend the night there and be back at the hospital in time for lunch the next day.

Their journey began in a blast of setting sunlight, the train drawing out of Charing Cross station and over the old iron railway bridge.

'It's like being in a film,' Salma said, and gave Ruth a winsome Bombay-Hollywood smile. 'Georgia Hale – The Gold Rush.'

The sun's rays flickered through the heavy girders, faster as the train gathered momentum. Ruth blinked behind her spectacles.

'No?' Salma took up another pose. 'Margaret Lockwood – The Lady Vanishes.'

'What?' Ruth mumbled.

'Never mind. Isn't it exciting? In twenty minutes we'll be in Woolwich. I'm sure you'll like the Macnair-Stuarts.'

Ruth stared out of the window. It was ages since she had travelled on a train. She had forgotten the smell, of soot and cigarette ash, and the prickly feel of the seats, the heat at the back of your legs.

'Peckham Rye,' Ruth shouted as the station sign flashed by. 'Muriel Spark, I think.'

'I beg you pardon?'

'I don't know, I've never read it.'

'Oh, I see.'

No you don't see, you don't see at all. But it doesn't matter; I don't mind.

They took a taxi to Fairview Close, not a nice London taxi-cab but a converted car with broken springs and crackling radio. The door was answered by a tall man in a green cardigan and mustard corduroy trousers, a sty in his right eye. He made no effort to speak, merely stared at them.

'Nurse Bekir,' Salma volunteered.

'Sorry, didn't recognise you without your uniform. Day off? Do come in. Ruth Harrison, isn't it? Pleased to meet you. This way. The wife's in here.'

He led them across a pleasantly decorated hall, their tread muffled by the autumnal carpet, and opened a door marked 'Private'. Ruth felt his hand in the small of her back propelling her towards a large lady in a motorised wheelchair. Mrs Macnair-Stuart pulled a lever on the arm of her chair and rolled to meet them.

'How do you do, dear,' she said, proffering her hand.

'How do you do.'

The touch was friendly, the voice warm. Ruth smiled.

'That's more like it. Laugh and the world laughs with you.'

'Frown and you sleep alone,' her husband responded, and to prove the point blew his wife a kiss.

Salma gave Ruth a told-you-so nod of encouragement. 'If you don't mind I'll be getting along,' she said. 'These are Ruth's things.' She put the Sainsbury's carrier bag down by Ruth's feet. 'You've got your ticket safe? Have a good time. See you tomorrow.' She patted Ruth on the elbow, and left.

From outside in the hall Ruth heard the beginnings of a whispered conversation between Salma and Mr Macnair-Stuart, and tried to listen. The wheel of Mrs Macnair-Stuart's wheelchair bumped against her toe.

'Never mind them. Now sit yourself down over here and tell me all about our Ruth. You're an artist, aren't you? Very talented, I'm told. Wish I could paint, must be lovely.'

3

Inside herself she smiled. From the expression on their faces –
shock on Salma's, surprise on Dr Tobias', shame on Mum's –
Ruth could tell she was giving quite a performance.

She pressed down on the horn again, and kept pressing. One
little second two little seconds three little seconds, she counted
in her head . . . sixty little seconds. Start again. One little
second two little seconds three little seconds . . . two minutes
. . . three minutes. At the end of five minutes she stopped, and
waited to see the reaction. Dr Tobias removed the fingers from
his ears and made a sign suggesting she wind down the window.
Ruth shook her head and gave a sharp 'toot-toot' to keep them
on their toes. A crowd had gathered, kids and housewives
standing by the hospital railings, patients and nurses on the
steps, all eyes fixed on the black Jaguar parked beneath the lime
trees.

'I want to g-o-o-o-o h-o-o-o-o-me,' she screamed. Realising
they could probably hear very little outside, she mouthed the
refrain: 'I need to. I n-e-e-d to.' With the car keys in her hand
and all four doors locked Ruth knew there was nothing much
they could do, short of breaking the windscreen.

Mrs Harrison took a faltering step towards the car but was
stopped by Dr Tobias' restraining arm. Dr Tobias said something. Mum frowned, staring at her daughter. They spoke
again. Mum turned and walked away across the potholed
hospital forecourt. Dr Tobias hesitated before following her.
And the two of them disappeared into the building.

Not long now. It won't be long now. Good old Mum.

Ruth blew on the lenses of her spectacles and rubbed them in the folds of a mohair stole Brigit had given her on Battle of Britain Day.

He'll have taken Mum into the consulting room and be blathering on about communal responsibility, the duty to share. No need to feel guilty, he'll be saying, it's our turn now.

Ruth smiled.

If he tries to make her sign one of those forms again she'll tear it up and throw it in his face! She *will*.

I could go on of course. Trying and failing. Getting better and worse then better again. Each time a little bit better, so they say. I could do it if I had to. If it wasn't for Mum I would, there'd be no choice. But to do it when I don't have to? How could anyone *choose* to live at the Glen Creran? I'd go mad in that room. Thinking of the Priory.

It's no use trying to be someone you're not. That's the mistake I've always made. Too many people have egged me on, told me how clever I am, how sensitive I am. Have said what a pity it is I shut myself away in my own world. Have encouraged me to think I could lead a normal life, should lead one.

It's not the doctors' fault, it's their job. It's nobody's fault. It's human nature to want everyone to be the same.

Actually I quite liked the Macnair-Stuarts. Her anyway. I liked the little white dog with a brown patch over one eye. Asleep on her knees. On an embroidered cushion. She had contacts in the Co-op, she said. She said she might be able to get me a job in the staff canteen, a proper job with a pay packet.

A few weeks ago there was nothing I wanted more in life than a pay packet.

Now I'll never have one. I'm going home.

Ruth caught sight of Mrs Callanan at a window of the Muriel Kenny Ward, and waved, leaning forward so she could be seen from the second floor.

It's me, Ruth. Can't you see? Down here.

Ruth rolled down the window and stuck out her arm, waving wildly to attract the old biddy's attention. Mrs Callanan slowly removed both hands from her dressing-gown pockets and gave Ruth a double thumbs-up sign.

There you are! She knows *exactly* what's going on, I knew she did. Why should she speak? What is there to say? In her time she's said it all.

It can't be easy being a doctor. Keeping up the pretence. Pretending all the time we're getting better, pretending we'd be any better off even if we were getting better. Knowing Mrs Callanan and me know they're only pretending.

You've got to accept things as they are.

That is to say: *I* have to accept things as they are.

Mum manages to go on believing it'll all be different every time, dreaming the same old dreams. Let her. I can't. Not any more. It's too painful.

Living with Bri in Glebe Place was always a dream.

I never thought it would be easy, knew it would be a struggle. Silly of me, playing their games. They're wrong, so very wrong. Give it a try, they say. Don't give up. It doesn't matter whether you succeed or not, just keep on trying. That's what matters, they say.

It's not them who fail, is it?

It's us who get hurt.

All Dr Cardy wanted me to do was paint. It took a long time before I was any good at it. He was right, though, I got there in the end, that's the point. How's your magnificent mother, he used to ask at check-ups. Dr Cardy really understands me and Mum. He knows a mother can't desert her child. She'll always go on hoping. She's got to.

Bri can't help herself when it gets bad. I was lucky, really, having as long as I did of her friendship. The time was always going to come, sooner or later, when she'd turn against me. In my heart of hearts I never expected anything else. Poor Bri. She'll never be able to go home. Not like Neil. Not like me.

I've got Mum. And Mum's got me. We're more than enough for each other. Who could want any more? It's wrong to want any more. And I don't, not any longer. It's for my greed, my failure to be satisfied with what I've got that God punishes me.

I love Mum so much, Goddi. Let me be with her, that's all I ask. I'll never leave her again, I promise. With Mum I'm safe, in the in-between.

Ruth stared at the polished rosewood dashboard in front of her nose, her small hands gripping the wheel, miles, years away. She didn't notice her mother approaching the car and was startled by the sharp tap of a jewelled knuckle on the driver's window. Mum was smiling. She had a pile of Ruth's clothes over one arm and three carrier bags in the other. Ruth unlocked the car door.

'Give us the key to the boot will you, dear? They're bringing your case. Anything else?'

'My head of Neil, in Occupational Therapy.'

'Yes, got that.'

'Can I say goodbye to Bri?'

'Must you? Couldn't you write?'

Ruth looked at her mother, saw the strain in those watery eyes, noticed a certain breathlessness. 'Yes, I'll write. That'd be best.'

Dr Tobias himself appeared carrying her suitcase. 'I'm sorry you're leaving like this,' he said, laying Ruth's case flat in the carpeted boot of the Jaguar. 'Is there no way I can persuade you to stay? We were just getting somewhere.' Ruth shook her head, refusing to speak.

'Goodbye, Mrs Harrison. Do see your GP about that angina. Take care.'

Standing by the car door, while Mum settled herself, Dr Tobias banged the roof in a friendly salute. At the second attempt they made it out through the iron gates of All Souls and turned left, right, then left again to join the westbound traffic on Roman Road.

'It's alright, they can't stop us now,' Mum muttered. Her head shook, wobbled, and the car stalled at the lights. 'I think,' she said as she re-started, 'I'll stop for a minute. Catch my breath.' And she escaped down a cul-de-sac, parking beside the railings of the municipal playground. 'There we are.' She reached for the handbag at her feet and extracted Dad's silver hip-flask. 'You only had to ask, you know. I wasn't sure you wanted to come home.'

'Oh, Mum! I told you dozens of times.'

Mum chuckled. 'Made it clear enough in the end,' she said.

At three in the afternoon they finally reached Shepton Mallet, and fifteen minutes later were driving down the deep green drive to the Priory. Ruth was unable to contain herself, a smile becoming a giggle and erupting into a roar of laughter.

'What's the joke?' her mother asked, also laughing.

'Nothing.'

There was no point in trying to explain; it was too compli-
cated, even for Mum. She would only take it as a criticism, and
it wasn't a criticism, it was a fact. The fact was that the drive had
become so overgrown with mosses and lichen it was barely a
drive, more of an avenue; more like one of those double-banked
avenues of ancient trees, walled off at one end, leading between
two ploughed fields to a small paddock where a farmhouse, or a
castle, might once have stood. It didn't matter. It really didn't
matter at all. Only it was important to admit that this was what
it was really like, not as she always saw it in her mind.

At the end of the drive the Priory itself stood. Alive, but
nearer to death than to birth. Much nearer. A long section of
iron gutter hung diagonally across the front of the house,
resting on the balcony of the entrance porch. The verandah roof
had caved in and the wisteria had forced its way through the
debris, eager fingers clutching at drainpipes, clawing at window
sills, hauling itself up the wall onto the roof. Ruth laughed
again. What else could she expect? It hadn't been cut for years,
not since Dad's death, in fact.

Mrs Cornish was waiting for them in the kitchen, a kettle on
the boil. She bustled them into the studio and sat them down on
the chaise longue, placing a tray of toast and tea between them
on a bamboo table.

'See you tomorrow, Ruthie dear,' she said at the door.
'Lovely having you home.'

Mother and daughter ate greedily, spooning home-made jam
straight onto their toast.

'Nice,' Mrs Harrison said, pouring herself a third cup. 'It'll
be like the old times now.'

'Which old times?'

'When you were painting dolls. The calm times. Remember?'

'Of course,' Ruth replied. 'I remember everything . . .'

Ruth smothered the words of disagreement as they formed,
guarding her thoughts. The calm times? Those were not calm
times. They were controlled, contained times, not calm times.
The calm times are coming now, now that I've stopped dreaming. I'm not going to try and dream things different any more.
The grass is never greener on the other side of any fence. It's
scorched bare in patches, rubbed earth-brown by traversing

feet, knotted with weeds and lichen, littered with cigarette packets. Nobody's worse or better off than anyone else; it's all the same.

There was no easy rhythm to Ruth's life at the Priory, as before. There were days, many days to begin with, when she was too weary to leave her room, whole mornings when tears poured from her eyes and sobs slipped out underneath her bedroom door and crept down the stairs to trouble her mother, listening in the hall.

'Don't fret so, Mrs H,' Mrs Cornish would say. 'A good cry never did no one no harm.'

Then five weeks, seven weeks once, could pass in concentrated daily labour in the studio, broken only to recite the sacred offices from her Confirmation Book of Common Prayer.

On one of their weekend outings from All Souls, Ruth and her mother had visited the British Museum. Ruth now spent much of her time in the studio with the postcards she had bought on this visit, reproducing on a large scale over and over again the same illuminated miniatures. A certain capital 'T' was her favourite, with King David kneeling in an enchanted garden plucking his psaltery, a unicorn and a lion peering round the trunk of a tree, God in the sky above surrounded by angels and gazing contentedly down. Of her previous paintings, 'The Martyr's Gate' was the only one she still valued: a profoundly religious work, the best I ever did, she told Neil in a letter. 'Thy Kingdom Come' was gone, forgotten, sold for two thousand pounds at the Royal Academy Summer Show while Ruth was in hospital.

Ruth's bouts of activity with the brush were interspersed with long days of reading and letter-writing. She especially enjoyed reading in the open air, and on some of the coldest days that winter was to be found lying in the hammock on the verandah of the gazebo, Dad's army greatcoat over her own duffel, thumbing familiar pages of *Tess*. In Dad's study in the evenings she liked to read at random from the *Encyclopaedia Britannica*, noting odd facts about which she wished to think more deeply, and transcribing pornographic snippets to amuse Neil. Samoan fisherboys, she was able to tell Neil in one letter, must have their penises tattooed before being allowed to make young love. The letters themselves she usually composed at the bureau in the studio. Ruth wrote to Brigit most weeks too, rambling letters about package holidays, the Theosophical Society, Ruskin's *Seven Lamps of Architecture*, anything except day-to-day matters of life with Mum on the rim of their Somerset village. Brigit's failure to reply did not deter Ruth, and at Christmas a card arrived from Staff Nurse Trudy Fellowes ('pp Lady Brigit Crighton') thanking her for her 'super' letters.

In Vancouver Graham Fitzgerald benefited from Ruth's new-found literary zeal, as did Mark, Sylvia, Pippa, Alice and James, collectively and individually. Jane Owen, a friend from school, now married and living in Pwllheli, received more-or-less monthly missives to which she responded with eager pages of backward-sloping gossip about the hotel in which she worked as a waitress. Dredging old diaries for missing contacts Ruth was overjoyed to come across the Prévert's address and immediately wrote in half-remembered French to 'Cher Madame et Monsieur', parents of Claude-Michel, the boy who had given her her first kiss, in a tree-canopied avenue of the Jardin des Plantes. To these and all her other correspondents, regular and occasional, Ruth was highly selective in what she told them of herself, her purpose in writing to prove that she could do so without making demands, without raising hopes or fears, to settle not stir, and to tell her friends what they needed to hear. Only to Uncle Gordon, plain Gordon as he had recently asked her to address him, did she dare from time to time unburden the fullness of her anxieties. Uncle Gordon, as she still preferred to think of him, was different from the rest: Uncle Gordon had suffered and survived; Uncle Gordon lived on his own on an immovable hulk in the Bay of Toulon; Uncle Gordon recited poetry on the lavatory; Uncle Gordon believed in God and feared nothing, neither in heaven nor on earth.

All the hours and every hour she could possibly spare from her other commitments, health and weather permitting, Ruth spent walking in the surrounding countryside. It was her one indulgence, she used to say, the only thing she allowed herself to do solely for personal pleasure. A harmless pleasure, surely? A pure pleasure.

Ruth skipped and sang down the final few yards of the path

through the spinney and scrambled over the stile. So many beautiful places to walk to, which would it be today? She looked up at the sky. Eleven o'clock, plus or minus: too late for the long walk down the Lee Farm side of the valley to the base of Glastonbury Tor and back across the sedgemoor, watchful of its shifting paths. Instead she might turn left up the heifers' sloping field, still empty this hard February, cross the road, and push her way through Heber Cut to the top of the ridge. And from there? Anywhere she liked. Down the other side to inspect Mr Gaunt's vineyard if she wanted to. Or she need not cross the road, but walk a quarter of a mile along, away from the village as far as the level crossing, and climb onto the grassed-over railway track to chase the rabbits. So many things she could do. She could look for mushrooms in the pylon field, beneath the humming wires. No, not today. Tomorrow perhaps. Today, at any rate, she could manage both her special walks before lunch. First, the crown of beeches.

Starting from the gate at the foot of the mound she walked clockwise – anti-clockwise in the afternoons – twice round the outside of the fence, beating the bent top-rails with a piece of rope knotted at one end. She sometimes missed, and stopped to aim again. Often the rope wound itself too many times around the rail to be released by its own reverse momentum and she had to pull hard to disengage it, dragging sections of the fence closer to the ground in the process. On admission to the crown itself her only further duty was to touch the trunk of each old tree. In any order; as many times as she felt they needed.

Who counted? *How* mattered, not how many. And that no one saw her, that was important too. Better to miss a day, several days, than be spotted arriving or leaving. Or, God forbid, actually doing.

Ruth loved the feel of those trees. She often rubbed her cheek against the rough bark, enjoying the friction between their two skins. She talked to them too, told them how beautiful they were, whispering sweet entreaties into lipped cracks in the tree-trunks.

There were no such pagan rituals about Ruth's other special walk, down around Dad's lake, the place she liked to be best, the place she always chose to go when she did not have to be anywhere else.

Dad's lake (or Mat's lake or Mr Harrison's lake) was what it was called because Dad's lake was exactly what it was. He had made it. By damming the stream at Watham Vale's shallow neck a few hundred feet before it flattened out to merge with the sedgemoor; with the company's bulldozers and queues of rubble dumping tip-up trucks making a terrible mess at the inhospitably wet end of their second summer at the Priory; against all the locals' advice. It had worked though, perfectly. Dad's perfect boating, fishing, bathing, shooting, skating lake. Dad's lake, now hers.

From the crown Ruth walked round through the fields to behind the barn and let herself onto the lake-path, flanked on one side by a sentinel line of poplars and on the other by the stream. A Saint Valentine's flock of magpies flirted and played, jumping from branch to branch, one and then another flying off in an almost graceful arc, showing off their shot plumage. Ruth loved to see the spring signs of sociability in these otherwise ill-mannered birds. The light gurgling sounds of the stream deepened and slowed, its firm banks giving way to reeds and, at the lake itself, to giant bulrushes. It was at this end, on either bank, that Dad and Mark had built for themselves reed-roofed shelters each year in which to hide and wait for the evening flights of duck. When Ruth accompanied them it had been her job to launch the decoys while the men scattered feed. Sitting in Dad's butt, her feet already ice solid, she had held her nose and manufactured quacking sounds at the back of her throat. It pained her now to think of those times, to recall the pride and excitement of being invited along, and the boasts and story-telling when they returned to Mum in the Priory kitchen. It hurt her to remember Dad's lethal calm as the first flight of the evening appeared in the red sky, five dots near the horizon, arrowing towards the pear-shaped stretch of water created with the approaching moment precisely in mind. Over their heads she again saw five mallard fly. 'Quack' they cried. 'Quack' she replied, turning them in a wide circle. The circle narrowing, the duck banking steeply in the predestined pattern. Lower and nearer they came. The click of Dad's safety catch. Finally, swiftly, the gun raised to his shoulder. 'Bang! Bang!' The splash of a small, warm dead weight falling in the water.

Ruth continued on along the path to the western shoulder of

the lake where the water curled back from the dam. Frogs'
Farm, as Mark and she had called this spot when young. It was
for all these memories Ruth came day after day, for the
reminders of things past, bad and good. Screaming, screaming:
'Don't! Don't! Oh please don't,' when the boys pulled mating
toads from the lake, and prised them apart, loosing the creatures' clasped arms with the blades of their pen-knives. 'Sissy'
the boys had shouted back, and had chased her up the path,
hurling toads at her retreating bottom. Ruth was a tough little
girl and ran fast, faster still since once having been caught and
having had handfuls of spawn stuffed down her shirt. Russell
Gaunt, she recalled, was the member of her brother's gang
she had most feared, the acknowledged master of childhood's
most disturbing skills. Eyes, for example: Russ was brilliant
at eyes. Without warning, in mid-conversation, he would roll
his eyes till the pupils disappeared leaving blank blue-white
orbs.

And the eyelid trick. Folding his eyelids inside out.

'Agh! Horrid!'

Ruth shook her head to dispel this latest image.

In the middle of Dad's lake was a small island with two
willows, a deserted swan's nest, and a mooring post once
painted green. Dad had had everything painted green. Or
black, like the yard door, and the Jaguar. She reached the
wooden landing-stage beside the brick sluice: six feet of clear
water into which their rain-filled rowing boat was threatening to
sink. Ruth stood at the end of the jetty and stared into the
mirror-black surface. 'Now, push yourself out with your feet
and reach down with your arms. There, that's better,' Dad had
said. Kindly at first, then more and more impatiently when she
consistently failed to enter the water head first. 'You can't be
trying. Go on, properly this time.' Ruth shivered in the sunshine, flopped in, and was hauled out again by the arm. 'Ow,
Dad. You're hurting me.' A smack on the cheek. 'Again.' She
could take it no longer and swam frantically away from the jetty,
doggy paddle all the way to the island, five times as far as she
had ever swum before. 'Ruth, come back immediately!' Silence. 'I'm waiting,' he shouted. And so he waited. And waited
– till nearly five-thirty when the Pembertons were due at the
crown for croquet, and he was obliged to leave his post.

Physically and emotionally exhausted on the return swim Ruth had twice felt herself slipping below the surface of Dad's lake, and twice had forced herself back into the world above, gasping for air, sobbing and whimpering as she reached out for the shore.

Ruth picked up a tiny ball of lead left behind by a trespassing angler and tossed it away into the distance. Too light to shatter the sheet of transparent ice, the lead ball bounced and bobbled towards the island, sending a trill of notes reverberating around the overgrown edges of the lake.

'There you are,' she told herself. And continued her walk.

With these special walks, her letter-writing and the new religious paintings, there was little time for anything else. Not that Ruth would have wanted anything else had there been the time. And no one seemed to expect anything more of her now either. Attacking Mum with a dustpan-brush, 'they' – the village, friends and family – could not ignore that, could not forget that; they were forced to accept the indelible evidence of agony stamped on Mum's face, the spider's web scar beneath the make-up on her temple, a damaged nerve fluttering her eyelid, the shadowy depression and gristly swelling on her skull. In attacking Mum, Ruth had attacked herself, had inflicted hidden wounds much deeper than the kitchen knife in her stomach. 'They' would never be shown these scars: she didn't expect them to understand, didn't want them to, had no wish to explain. Ruth Harrison had beaten her mother over the head with the back of a dustpan-brush, had beaten her mother so hard and so many times that she had sprained her wrist. Ruth's mother had been beaten unconscious by her own daughter in her own bed, spattering blood on the bedside lampshade. The facts spoke for themselves. Unable to avoid the facts, they avoided Ruth; and Ruth avoided them, happy to shed the intolerable burden of others' hopefulness.

There were the odd exceptions, though; there were bound to be the odd exceptions. Like Mrs Fitzgerald. And Polly Jeason, the weaver's wife. Polly had called round at the Priory one afternoon shortly before Christmas, in floods of self-pitying tears.

'God, we're all so blind. I know exactly what you must've

been feeling. Why didn't I speak my mind? Is it fear? If only you'd said something to me, Ruthie. We were such friends. It could all so easily be avoided. All this, this fighting, all this jealousy and stupidity. Oh God, I can't find the words. I won't let you do anything like that again. Look, let's . . .' on and on Polly talked, crying and laughing, squeezing Ruth's hand.

Poor Polly. Never right; without ever being entirely wrong.

Mrs Fitzgerald pitied no one, least of all herself. 'I'm surprised your mother took you back,' she said to Ruth on one visit, as they walked slowly up and down the drive. 'Not sure she should've done, as a matter of fact.'

'Why not?'

'Why should she? After what you did.'

'Because she's my mother.'

'That's no excuse.'

Why was Twinkle so kind to her, that was what Ruth *really* wanted to know. Twinkle's capacity for accepting anything and everything she did astonished Ruth. Of accepting without question, without surprise, without desire. With love and with loyalty, never demanding anything in return.

'Don't you expect *anything* of me – at all? Ever?' Ruth asked.

'Your friendship, that's all.'

'And I've never disappointed you?'

'No.'

'*Never?*'

'It's your life, Jo, not mine.'

'You expect a lot of yourself though.'

'That's different.'

'Is it? I don't want anything any more. My life's ambitionless.'

'So?'

'So I accept my limitations.'

'We've no choice.'

'Yes, I know. But I didn't know. I thought everything was possible.

'Everything *is* possible, of course. Not for everybody, though. That's the point. I've got to make do with what I've got, which is quite a lot. I don't fight the awfulness any more. When it comes I accept it. I know there's nothing I can do. That's a comfort in itself. A release. Knowing there's no solution. Knowing I must suffer. World without end.'

'That's news?' Twinkle queried.

'To me it is, yes.'

4

Long letters, yes, and the occasional telephone call, but actually coming to stay? Surely not. That had never been part of the plan; there was too much to do. No, she was far too busy for visitors.

'But what did he say, Mum? When's he coming? This is *impossible*.'

'It'll be a nice change, dear.'

'Nice? You've never met him. It won't be nice at all, it'll be horrid. Why did you say yes? I'm not having anything to do with him. I won't, I promise. I'll lock myself in my room. I *will*.'

'I, I thought . . .'

'Oh, Mum!'

The look of bewilderment on her mother's face, replacing the pleasure with which she had reported the news of Neil Skinner's Easter visit, was more than Ruth could bear; she covered her head with her arms, like a boxer on the ropes, and groaned.

'Please, Ruthie, don't. I'll put him off. Please don't make that noise, it breaks my heart. I only did it for you.'

Ruth had dropped onto a corner of the old settee next to the kitchen range, and was rocking backwards and forwards, head still covered. Mum sat down beside her, trying to pull Ruth's arms away from her contorted face.

'I thought Neil was your friend,' she coaxed.

'He is, I *love* Neil. But I don't want to see him. I don't want to see anyone. Won't you understand?' Ruth whined.

'You don't have to, dear.'

Ruth abruptly ceased her mournful rocking, and through the

fleshy bars of her arms asked more calmly: 'What did he say exactly?'

'Nothing. Just asked what we were doing at Easter. It's only four days. He'll be in church most of the time.'

'If he isn't a Buddhist by then.'

This remark elicited a chuckle from Mum. Ruth flung her arms about her mother's neck, the two of them falling across the settee.

'Ooh!'

'I love you. I love you so much, Mum.'

'How much?'

'A hundred.'

'My, that's a lot.'

They lay there quietly, Ruth with her head buried in a cushion pinning her mother down with the combined weight of body and soul.

'If I keep him out of your way during the day, can he come then?' Mum finally asked.

'If he wants to. I don't care. He can do whatever he wants.'

'You don't mind? Really?'

'No, I don't mind.'

When Neil arrived by coach on the Thursday evening, at the Clock Tower in Shepton where Mr Cornish had been dispatched to meet him, Ruth was already in bed. The next morning Mrs Harrison walked Neil over to Holy Communion at Eastney. After the service she introduced him to Reverend Hibbs who had promised to look after the young convert on the Saturday, Good Friday itself being a day for private contemplation, Ruth had declared.

One way and another she managed to avoid more than a passing word with her friend from All Souls until supper time on the Saturday.

'Good bloke, your vicar,' Neil was saying. 'Knows a lot.'

'What about?'

'About you.'

'*Me?*'

Neil laughed, and rubbed his fingers through his greasy ginger hair, much longer now than it had been in hospital. 'Not you particularly. People in general.'

'Oh.' Ruth allowed herself a laugh too.

'What news of Brigit?' Neil asked.

'No better.'

'No? What's she say?'

'Doesn't. She never writes.'

'That's the way it goes,' he muttered.

'Will you be alright in London?' Ruth asked, suddenly feeling protective of him again. She stroked his knee.

'Hope so. No good if I can't do it up there too.'

'God'll help.'

'Yeh, couldn't do it without Him. I owe you for that, Ruthie.'

'You owe God, not me.'

'True. Hey, who's that bloke working in your field? Does *he* drink?'

'What do you mean?'

'On the bottle. You haven't noticed? The young bloke? Was yesterday for sure. Or else he's barmy. Dancing around like a scalded cat.'

'There's no one working in our fields. Must've been a tramp.'

'Leave off! Planting bloody trees he was.'

'He was not!' Ruth shouted.

'Okay. I was seeing things. Ruth, look, it's okay. I made a mistake.'

Someone *was* there, though. There had been someone working in the paddock for the last three weeks, and she knew his name – Jonathan Pollard.

Jonathan Pollard.

It was a good name, a strong yet sensitive name. If only he'd done a bit more work he'd have got a first. This job with Gerry Boynton was a temporary escape, a rest from his research. The leasing of their paddock to Gerry's landscape garden business was only temporary too; Mum might want another donkey. A few experimental trees wouldn't do any harm, would they? Quite the opposite. You could hardly see the paddock anyway, hidden behind the hedge.

If only I didn't know his name I could pretend he wasn't there.

'It might have been one of Gerry Boynton's men, I suppose,' Ruth admitted.

'Not worth a quarrel whoever he is. Look, let's forget about it, shall we?'

That's what I've been trying to do, forget. You can't, though, not by force. Forgetfulness comes to you, you don't go to it. You have to wait and be patient. Remembering to forget doesn't work.

Step by step it has to be, with tests along the way. This Jonathan Pollard is one of my tests, and I mustn't be so hysterical about it. Mustn't be afraid.

What is there to be afraid of? He's only a boy working in our paddock. That's all. A crazy boy with a motorbike. He's nothing to do with me, so why do I have to pretend he doesn't exist?

'Sorry, Neil. I wonder if supper's ready yet?'

'R-u-u-th. Supper,' Mum called through to the studio from the green baize door. 'In the dining room.'

After lunch on the Thursday of Easter Week – falling early that year, on St Ambrose's Day, she had noted that morning in her ecclesiastical calendar – Ruth decided to bicycle over to Evercreech and call on Polly Jeason. On the Tuesday, Neil had returned for his last few months at the rehabilitation home in Poole, looking well – all the better for seeing her, he had said. Ruth felt guilty about Polly, guilty for being so cautious and uncommunicative, so mean to a friend in need. It was time to make amends.

'Shoo! Get off.'

Two of Mum's hens fluttered from the handlebars of her bicycle.

'Naughty girls.'

Ruth spat on her handkerchief and wiped the saddle clean.

What a heavenly day.

She pedalled slowly up the dark drive, gazing between the conifers at the cattle munching in the sun. A beast scratched her aerated belly against a post of the fence, and clumps of primrose floated, like lilies, on the mossy earth. Ruth was halfway along the drive before she noticed a figure standing at the gateless centre of the eyebrows, the tall green and yellow figure of a man. She pedalled on up the hill, dismounting in the shadow and pushing her bicycle through onto the sunlit stage. It was a

boy not a man, with plumb-straight corn-coloured hair hanging
to the padded shoulders of his army surplus sweater. A young
man really, not a boy, with a narrow face and a wonderful nose,
the shape of a flat-iron, like the prow of a steamer.

'Hello,' he said.

'Hello,' she instantly replied.

'Hello, hello, anyone at home?' And he laughed, royally.
'Never mind.'

'I don't.'

'What a day. What a miraculous day. Intoxicating.'

'Pardon?'

'I'd very much like to see your current work sometime.
Would you mind? Any time'll do, just give us a shout. 'Bye for
now.' With his long legs he stepped up onto the curved wall.
'Alright?'

'Fine. I'll give you a shout.'

'Good,' he said as he pushed through a hole in the hawthorn
hedge and wandered off into the paddock.

So that's Jonathan Pollard.

Love his nose!

Polly and Ruth sat and talked in the gallery of St Columba's
Evercreech; sculpted squirrels played around the capitals and
two chattering monkeys clambered up a pilaster.

'That's him over there. See?'

'Where?'

'There. The gargoyle stroking his conk.'

'Ruth really! It's nothing like Marty.'

'Not Martin. Jonathan.'

'Jonathan who?'

'Pollard. I bumped into him on the way.'

'Oh *him*!'

Standing one perilously wet morning of the following week at
the window of Dad's study, Ruth caught sight of Jonathan
Pollard crouched beneath the big cedar at the bend in the drive.
He was hugging his legs to his chest, chin resting on his knees.
Eighty yards away through the swirling rain she felt his gaze
upon her, safe in the Priory's squat flint tower.

Better let him in. Poor boy, must be soaked to the skin.

Ruth turned from the window, singing to herself, and went downstairs into the hall. The ecclesiastical front door was bolted and locked; she pulled it open to find Jonathan already standing there in the shelter of the carriage porch, puffing at a newly-lit cigarette, water-darkened hair pressed flat to his head.

'Rescued at last,' he chuckled.

Seems to laugh a lot. Sounds nice.

'You're wet.'

She led him into the kitchen, made him take off his socks and sweater, and gave him a gigantic orange bathtowel with which to dry his hair. He stood and steamed in front of the Aga. And talked, how he talked: she had never heard anyone talk like that – in declamatory bursts of personal revelation, an enchanting fusion of poetry and opinions and information. In a single breath, it seemed, he detailed his father's premature retirement from Gray's Inn, the family's move a year before to Pilton, and the pleasures of part-time landscape gardening. Unable, and unwilling, to interrupt, Ruth frowned in sympathy with his missed first, and applauded his passion for Arthurian Romance. On and on he talked, praising Russian Expressionism, condemning Dada, eschewing politics. He hummed Bizet, quoted Verlaine and criticised C. P. Snow.

'I am Pollard, is how I'll begin,' he said, presaging his lectoral return in triumph to Cambridge. 'In pink socks and sandals, like old Southwood. Or was it bare foot-flesh, we ask, frost-stained in the march along Grange Road from his prehistoric digs? Those famous Southwood dashes across the podium, grunting and gesticulating like a Kabuki prima-donna. You should've seen him, haring back to the desk to consult the next card. Stage directions!' Jonathan roared his appreciation of the memory. 'Ha, ha! Aha ha! Minute stage directions, you see? Not lecture notes at all!'

Ruth smiled, and nodded, expecting him to dance away into another field of thought, another story.

'Stage directions, see?' he repeated.

'Yes, very amusing.'

'Amusing! You think it's funny? Christ, it's a tragedy. The lunatic. An empty room he spouted at in the third term. A nude room. How much can a man take? Year after year they made him do the bloody course. I kept him company as long as I could. Actually, I got the giggles in the end and didn't dare go back.'

All the time these jolting changes of mood, and of language. So inconsistent, so uncertain of himself, his slender hands ingrained with dirt, both thumbs blistered. The third gentleman of Verona, as he used to see himself, he said.

Only a boy, really. A clever boy with a nose like a slice of cheese. A sensitive boy doing his best to please.

'Won't you show me your work?' he asked.

'If you want. But it's not what you think.'

'What do I think?'

'I don't know. Whatever you've been told, I suppose.'

'That you're unreliable, shall we say? No more than me I bet, and I was a school prefect. Second Head of House.'

'What do they say about my pictures?'

'I've seen one at Sandra Fare's. I was frightened it might fall off the wall. Still-life, eh? No sirree.'

'It's all different now. Come on.'

Ruth in her black dancing pumps, and Jonathan in a borrowed pair of shooting socks, tiptoed reverentially one behind the other to the studio.

These days Ruth worked at neither of her easels but at a spider-legged wallpapering table purchased at the DIY store in Shepton. Half a dozen works in progress were laid out along its narrow hardboard top, six identical pictures unfinished at precisely the same stage, the eyes, stigmata and genitals of each Christ fully realised, his flesh a flat wash of underpaint, the patterned background of swooping angels finely sketched in pencil, and the solitary beseeching figure of Mary Magdalen outlined in red paint at the foot of every cross.

Ruth's other paintings, the illuminated initials, twenty or thirty of them, were pinned with brass tacks to the balustrade of the minstrel's gallery.

Neither spoke. Jonathan walked slowly past the table and over to the gallery, extracting his last cigarette and tossing the empty packet onto the floor. He bit on the tip of the unlit cigarette. His eyes smiled.

'They must be nice to do,' he said.

Ruth stared at him.

'Mind if I play the piano?'

She shook her head. Jonathan lifted the stack of dried bulrushes from the keyboard, loosened the fitted blanket and opened the lid. Stooping to the keys, blonde hair curtaining his face from Ruth's stare, he began to play Chinese Chopsticks with two fingers, in extra-slow time at first, increasing the tempo at each refrain until he finally made a mistake, stopped, laughed, lit his cigarette.

'Out of practice,' he said, and laughed some more.

He understands. The boy understands. No explaining, no justifying, without my minding whether he does or not. He really does. Jonathan Pollard! What a funny fellow you are.

'Incidentally, I know where you got it from.'

'Got what?'

'The crucifix.'

Silly boy. Whatever will he say next?

'From the Baptist Church in Avalon,' Jonathan continued. 'Saint John's. You knew it once belonged to Judge Jeffreys? Yes indeed, it was in the hanging judge's wee hand when the Peeler reprimanded him on Wapping Steps. Saw him quartered in the Tower; heard the ravens bleat.'

'Jonathan, *please*. Do talk sense.'

'I am. Haven't you seen it? I'll show you on Sunday. And not Jonathan if you don't mind. Nor Jonty or Johnnie or Nat. Nothing like that.'

'I'll call you Boy.'

'If you wish. Boy's fine.'

Boy Pollard. The Boy. Oh yes, that'll be fine. Fine's just the word, thank you.

On Sunday, riding pillion on his motorcycle, Ruth spent the afternoon with Boy Pollard in Glastonbury, Avalon, as he consistently referred to the town. He first showed her the twelfth-century ivory crucifix in the crypt of St John's, collecting a key from the sexton's cottage in Badon Street. He took her to the common graveyard in Paradise; the location, he believed, of La Beale Isoud's burial pyre, and to a field on the eastern flank of the Tor where Sir Bedivere's hermit might once have lived. They inspected the remains of last summer's excavations at the lake-village outside Godney and returned to marvel at the hammered bronze bowls in the Museum. They argued and laughed, and treated themselves to a cream tea at Dunstan's Oven.

'Where myth and history mingle you have to trust your instinct a lot of the time or you never get anywhere at all,' Jonathan explained. 'A medievalist must have an instinct for the truth.'

'What about Sir Ector le Chalibaille and the Priory then?'

Jonathan wiggled his magnificent nose with an air of scholarly concentration.

'On balance, I'd say yes.'

'Yes what?'

'Yes everything.'

'Boy!'

'*Yes*, I said. Yes, I think the story's basically true. A crown of beeches doesn't merely happen. A crown of beeches like yours has a purpose in life. Only the ordinary things merely happen. You, me, Avalon, the crown, Frank Lloyd Wright, *we* all have a reason. Brave Sir Ector's mausoleum? Feels right to me.'

'The original priory up on the crown? How do you know?'

'Instinct,' Jonathan replied, and tapped his nose. 'Afraid I've run out of funds, could you pay for tea? Dinner next time. On me.'

To Ruth's constant surprise and happiness, with Jonathan there was always a next time. Next time, he would say, we'll go to the White Hart or next time I'll show you Stourhead. He was always showing her things, things she thought she'd seen before but discovered through him she had never seen at all; and telling her things, about himself and herself, as though he were both of them. Between the last time and the next time, time didn't exist.

He'll be gone soon. When the summer's over he'll go away and never come back. I want him to go. I want you to take him away, Goddi, I do. Before my love dies.

It will die won't it? Or be killed.

He's only a boy. He'll grow up and I won't be allowed to love him any more. It's better he goes now.

Poor Boy. I wish I could help him. He's such a clever boy, he could do so much if only. No. No 'if onlys'.

I'll tell him though, before he goes. It'd be a pity for him not to know.

The joy of love is too short and the sorrow thereof and whatever cometh thereof dureth over long.

Not *my* love, my love. Not mine, my Goddi.

They were sitting at the top of a steep grassy bank close to the point where Heber Cut emerged from Parse Wood; it was the middle of a cloudless September day. Ruth gathered into Mum's wicker hamper the discarded remains of their picnic, while Jonathan smoked.

'Next time it'll be London. I'll wine you at Zanzibar, dine you at the Garrick and whisk you back to my penthouse maisonette in, in Rutland Gate shall we say? Toddling distance from Horrids, you'd like that, wouldn't you? Say you will, Girl. Say you'll be mine, next time?'

He paused and opened one eye.

'Sir Tristram, the second most valiant knight in Christendom, had it away with his uncle's first wife for most of Malory. Why should I be denied?'

Ruth's back was turned. She was higher up the slope than Jonathan, several yards away, kneeling in the grass. There was no response.

'Ruth? Are you alright?'

No movement. Not a sound. And then very quietly, each word separately enunciated: 'I want to marry you.'

As she spoke, she raised her hand to silence his reply.

'I've always wanted to marry you. I wasn't going to tell you. I shouldn't be now, I know, but I can't help it. I've got to give you my love, Boy, I've got to. You need it, you'll see.

'I won't get in the way. I'll stay at home all day doing the cooking and mending your sweaters. You won't know I'm there. And you'll be able to work then, all the time. In the libraries. I won't mind how long or how late or how many years it takes. It doesn't matter because with me you'll get there in the end, I know you will. You don't believe me, but it's true. They'll make you a Professor.'

Ruth raised her head from her chest and turned to confront Jonathan where he still lay, hiding his eyes.

'Boy? Look at me, Boy. Please, I need to know. Will you marry me one day?'

5

Was I right? I wasn't wrong, was I?

There was nothing else I could do. And you didn't try to stop me, did you, Goddi?

I had to, for his sake. He wouldn't have believed I love him. He said so. He did. Didn't you hear him?

It's what we wanted anyway, for the crazy boy to take my love away with him. It's no use to me, never was; and he needed it.

Do you know what'll happen to my love now?

I suppose you do.

Wouldn't you tell me for once? It won't upset me, I promise. I'm interested, that's all.

I tell *you* everything.

I'll even tell you what I did with Jonathan, if you're interested. I *will*.

You didn't see that, did you, Goddi?

No, you missed that.

I knew it the moment I saw him, the moment he opened the studio door. Women have a kind of instinct for these things, you see. 'Oh, it's you,' I said, as though nothing had happened. 'Yes, it's me,' he said.

He had his safari suit on, and snub-nosed shoes with buckles. I wore white. There could be no more next times, we both knew that. This was the very last next time.

He ordered a bottle of Nuits St Georges, to celebrate the summer, and we sat by the river till the sun sank behind the Tor. The veal chops couldn't have been tastier, and they prepared a special dish of braised celery for me, because I love it so much. 'You're Jonathan now, I'm afraid, not

Boy,' I told him. 'I suppose I'll have to be,' he replied.

I wasn't at all frightened – you aren't with someone you trust, with someone you know as well as I know Jonathan Pollard. He spilt raspberry sorbet on his tie. On his blue silk shirt. On the lapels of his fancy jacket.

He parked his motorbike in the lane and we walked up the drive. There were lights on in the house, and pop music blared from a bedroom window. We could see Mr Boynton and Gerry playing snooker in the games room, shutters open to the mild September evening. Jonathan held my hand while I patted the snuffling head of a labrador. We kept close to the rhodo-dendrons to avoid being seen, and pushed through the newly painted door into the kitchen garden. My golden Gothic letters shone in the moonlight: Landscaping To The Gentry Limited.

The greenhouse was hot. Like a Swedish sauna bath, I imagine.

I love the sounds in a big greenhouse, don't you? At night it's wonderful. Trapped moths banging their heads all along the roof. Water trickling, you don't know where. Plants growing.

Poor Jonathan, he was a little tipsy. And nervous; as though his was the maidenhead. I undid my dress myself, and spread it out on the needles of a giant cactus. He said I was beautiful, the most beautiful creature he had ever set eyes on. A goddess, he called me.

Actually, I thought he'd have managed something better than that. I was surprised at that. Disappointed, really.

He was so gentle with me. His hands. His lips. His feet. Such gentleness. So wet, the sweat dripping from our naked bodies. So sweet too, drinking the milk at my breasts. He finished before I did but I couldn't let him go, it was so lovely.

You'll never know how lovely it is. That's one thing you can never know.

The second time he hurt me, yes that's true. They were different hands, clawing hands. And biting teeth.

I might have died.

He was snoring when I left him, lying on his back snoring; fingers covering his eyes, nose in the air.

The Word comes riding on a white horse, doesn't it?

The swift white horse has eyes of flame and its tongue is a sword which smites evil people to the ground, cuts off their limbs. If you haven't got the seal of God branded clear on your forehead the locusts will eat you. You can't escape: men shall desire to die and death shall flee from them.

Only you know how much I've suffered, Goddi. Only you know how many days and nights, how many months and years of days and nights I've gnawed my tongue in pain. How much longer? What more do I have to do?

He that believeth in me though he were dead yet shall he live. You said that, it's in the Bible. Whosoever liveth and believeth in me shall never die. You said that too.

I love you, Goddi, like no one else.

You could have stopped him if you'd wanted to, couldn't you? Maybe you did. Perhaps I've got it all wrong.

Maybe you stopped them all.

Did you?

I can't be sure any more. I'm not sure of anything any more. Only of you, Goddi. At least I can be sure of you.

A work bench stood against the far wall of the barn, oil-stained and worn, with a large mechanic's vice screwed to one end. Some tools lay scattered on the bench; a red bowsaw, quite new but without a blade, two rusty chisels, a monkey wrench, some dirty rags, a can of nutless bolts, a partly extended jack, several spark-plugs, and a blacksmith's hammer. Ruth picked up the hammer and pressed its rounded head into the palm of her hand. She tested its weight, tapping the vice, ringing metal on metal. Her mind evidently made up, she concealed the hammer beneath her cardigan and walked back across the yard to the kitchen.

'Goodness, such a hurry-flurry,' said Mrs C as Ruth brushed past her in the pantry passage, sending the green baize door swinging.

In the hall Ruth checked her step, crossed to the studio, opened then closed the door with a deceitful bang and tiptoed back to the other side of the hall, letting herself quietly into the drawing room. Safely inside, she turned the key in the lock.

It was twilight in the drawing room, yellowing blinds drawn; and dusty, smelling of settled dust; and, apart from the creak of the floorboards and the dancing uneven feet of the tambour writing desk she touched in passing, silent. On a carved hardwood plinth at the far side of the room stood a four-foot-tall porcelain vase. Ruth ran at the vase, the hammer raised above her head. Stopped; licked her lips. Reaching for a cushion she held it against the shoulder of the vase and swung the hammer in a wide arc, thudding into the cushion. In slow motion, like a dynamited skyscraper, the vase fell in pieces on the carpet.

'That's the way, that's the way,' she crowed.

At the centre of the mantelpiece sat a Meissen pagodaman, the ridiculous wide-mouthed smile frozen on his oriental face. Ruth sidled up to him and poked his exposed stomach with her hammer. The hinged hands fluttered. The nodding head shook. She smashed the hammer down on his bare skull. In quick succession, with sweeping ill-aimed blows, she switched her attack from a pipe-playing shepherdess, to Europa and the garlanded bull, over to a pair of Chelsea lovers and two parrots ranged across the top of a tallboy.

'That's the way.'

She was panting now. Saliva flecked her chin and cheeks. A splinter of porcelain had grazed her forehead and a trickle of blood descended in steps from furrow to furrow, disappearing into the thick black hair of an eyebrow.

Stopping to catch her breath she heard Mum's frantic call in the hall.

Dad's cutglass decanters stood on a tray with ancient bottles of Bitter Lemon, India Pale Ale, and some upended tumblers. Ruth put down her hammer and lifted up the oval tray with both hands.

'Would you care to help yourself? Lovely Amontillado I'm told. Don't worry, there's plenty more beer in the cellar.'

Returning to the fireplace she tilted the tray above the spiky brass fender and saw the contents slide to the edge; pushed by the weight from behind they toppled and fell, perishing in pieces at her feet.

Mum's whimper at the door and her hopeless rattling of the handle were replaced by the crunch of Mrs Cornish's shoulder into the woodwork, grunting as the air was forced in a rush from her lungs.

'Don't be silly now, dearie. Let us in. We won't do you no harm,' she shouted through the keyhole.

Where was the carriage clock, in its tooled Moroccan leather case with a slide that you pulled up to see the time and a special place at the top you pressed to hear it chime? There, on the sofa-table. Ruth picked it up and threw it as hard as she possibly could at the ceiling-high mirror above the fireplace.

'There you are!' she shouted, hooting with laughter.

She had missed the mirror. The carriage clock had bounced back off the wall and lay on its side beneath a chair, ringing the hours. All the hours, one following another without interval . . . dong dong dong dong . . .

I didn't know. No one told me. How can you know if no one tells you?

No one is ever able to tell anyone anything. We have to learn it all ourselves or not at all. That's the rule.

I am, I'm far too intense. Even with you, Goddi.

With me everything always has to be the *most* beautiful, the *most* holy, the *most* unhappy. Always the mostest. I laugh louder and longer and more often than anyone he's ever known; the loudest and oftenest laugher in Christendom. It's embarrassing sometimes, he said.

Why didn't somebody tell me before?

I didn't know.

I take everything so seriously, not just the big things, the little things too. Everything. Why does it matter so much more to me than to anyone else? I cry if, if a cow crushes a mushroom. When a silly heifer stepped on a mushroom once, I cried.

I don't blame him. He's right, it's impossible to share with someone like me.

I'll have my baby, though. At least he left me my baby.

You don't mind, do you, Goddi? Funny, I never thought of asking you before. Perhaps you do mind?

You needn't. It's nothing personal, you see. I call it my baby, but it's not mine really, it's yours. Don't you want your baby?

You can always take it back. Throw it away. Cast it into the bottomless pit of perdition. Feed its tender flesh to your seven-headed avenger. Do whatever you like, I don't mind.

Where shall I go? I can feel him kicking.

Not too far. Mum wouldn't want me too far away.

What I'd really like, what I'd like most of all, is to be the art teacher at Sherborne. It's a bit of a dream job, I know, but you've got to try for the top first. I can always lower my sights later. I think I'd get it anyway. I mean, not many people have had pictures on the line four years running, have they? And Dad being a governor is bound to help.

I'm not afraid.

I'll make them give me one of those pretty cottages down by the river, with a summerhouse in the garden where I can paint. One holiday every year, Easter probably, I'll go to stay with Uncle Gordon and imbibe the Mediterranean. My favourite pupil will join me there and we'll visit Aix for the day, share a French bread picnic in Cézanne's atelier.

Not every year. There won't be anyone good enough every year, I don't suppose. And even if there was I wouldn't necessarily like her. I'm not going to be a martyr to my students, you know.

I might marry. A master from the boys' school.

It wouldn't be right to have my baby at home.

It's not their talking I'd mind, but having to listen. To explain.

Art teachers are allowed babies on their own.

Then Mum could move. To a smaller house in the village. That's all she's ever wanted really. If it hadn't been for me.

And Dad.

'Mr Harrison-Sayers?'

'Yes?'

'I'm sorry,' Ruth whispered. 'It was meant to be a surprise.'

She stood propped up by a policeman at the front door of The Dower, a squad-car's blue light flashing at her back.

'Ah, she is your sister, sir.'

'Yes. She is. Darling,' Mark called up the stairs. 'Could you come, it's Ruth . . . Shall I?'

'Careful, Miss. There, that's more like it.'

'My God, what's happened?' Sylvia took Ruth from Mark, guided her through into the kitchen and sat her down on a chair. 'Now let's have a good look at you.'

Ruth remained motionless exactly where she found herself, perched on the edge of a Windsor chair at the black and white tiled centre of Sylvia's immaculate kitchen. She smiled.

'I could collect Pippa from school, couldn't I?'

She raised her head. It was difficult to see clearly as one of her spectacle lenses was broken, star-crazed like a shattered wind-screen. Someone was running water in the sink.

'I'm afraid I've put on rather a lot of weight in hospital. It doesn't really fit any more.'

She plucked at the tight sleeves of her tweed suit. The zip on her skirt was broken, the waistband inadequately secured by two safety pins; she played with the protruding tails of her blouse. A whiff of Dettol reached her from the sink.

'Aren't you going to tell me what happened?' Sylvia asked.

'They never let me have any money. So I had to hitchhike. I'm sorry, I didn't want to bother anyone, you see. That's why.'

'And?'

A pause, not long, before Ruth replied. 'It was a man in a car took me to the police. A nice man. He thought I was crazy, I think.'

Sylvia placed the plastic basin of warm water on the floor at Ruth's feet, and with a flannel began to wipe the grime from her face.

'I must've frightened him.'

'Here, put your feet in the water.'

Slipping off her shoes Ruth dipped her bare toes into the blue basin.

'Ooh!'

'Too hot?'

'No, lovely. Thanks.'

Ruth heard the front door bang shut, and looked up for Mark at the kitchen door. The expression on his blinkered face told her all she needed to know.

'It's all sorted out. I'll take her back myself,' he said to his wife, and left the room.

Ruth was lying fully clothed on the top of her own bed in her own little room at the back of the Priory. The curtains were open and the moon shone brightly in onto the narrow bed drawn tight against the window; her loose black hair curled onto the pillow framing her pale face.

Earlier she had rearranged the books on her chest of drawers, placing them in order, the largest at the centre, each volume precisely in line, securely contained between the bowed heads of Dad's elephant bookends. A small chequered case with pink carrying strap stood on the floor near the wardrobe, newly packed.

Everything was ready.

There was nothing more she could do.

Her breathing had slowed with the waiting and she gazed calmly out into the darkness towards the unseen line of poplars and through their leafless branches to the ruined chapel on the Tor. She smiled, remembering the nameless woman milking her goat and St Michael balancing souls, those two ill-matched figures up there on the wall above the western door.

The time had almost come.

Ruth sat up on the bed and swung her legs to the ground, feeling with her toes through brown woollen stockings the folded edges of Miss Pilk's rag rug. She walked across the room, lifted the latch and listened. She smiled again, and had to press a hand to her mouth to stop herself laughing out loud. The house was full of friendly sounds echoing across the years. Of course it was! What had she expected to hear? Nothing?

With a guiding hand on the banister she made her way down the stairs in the dark, and entered the studio. Everything was prepared. Wellington boots and duffel coat lay hidden beneath the chaise longue, her Prayer Book and the pair of precious wooden dolls set out in their tattered finery on the duet stool.

What else?

Nothing else. It was too late for anything else.

She was trembling now, and expelling breath in sharp sobs. For a moment, more than a moment, she faltered, stood swaying and rocking, eyes tightly closed, clutching the martyred dolls to her breast.

'I can't. I can't, Mum. Not again. I love you, you know that. I'm going now, Mum. He's calling me. I've got to go now . . . Please. Let me be.'

These last whispered words descended to a low moan as she stumbled to the French windows, and let herself out onto the verandah.

Ruth steadied herself, taking deep breaths of cold air, and stepped slowly into the darkness. Adjusting her eyes to the light of the moon, she saw the chickenwire fence first. Then the spinney. Further? Yes, there it was, there was the crown of beeches.

Coming, Goddi. I'm coming.

PART
IV

Seventeenth of January. After you are told certain things, sometimes long after, you realise you already knew them.
I was fast asleep when the telephone rang.
'Graham, is that you?'
'Speaking,' I said.
'Gray, this is Mrs Harrison. I thought you'd want to know, that Ruth died last night.'
'Died? Oh no, no, no.'
I kept saying 'no'. I can't think why. It was quite the stupidest thing to say.
'Yes, I'm afraid so. We found her this morning in the lake.'
'No, how awful.' I was sobbing shamelessly.
'And you, how are you?' I finally managed to ask.
'Thank you, I'm fine. I know she's at peace.'
Ruth's mother hesitated before going on.
'If only you could see her now. You couldn't refuse her now, Gray.
'She's never looked so beautiful.'